The Sword of Lumina: Mira's Last Book 3

by

Erin Elliott

F & I
by Melange Books

Published by
Fire and Ice
A Young Adult Imprint of Melange Books, LLC
White Bear Lake, MN 55110
www.fireandiceya.com

Mira's Last ~ Copyright © 2015 by Erin Elliott

ISBN: 978-1-68046-071-1

Cover Art by Caroline Andrus

To my brothers, Dustin and James.
For your assistance in the development of stories
through lifelong practice.
I wouldn't be the twisted person I am without you.

Prologue

Darkness. A cover for all that is false and cruel. The representation for lies and betrayal. In its most profound depths, will make a seeing man, blind. It brings fear to the stout hearted and causes the young to weep. Evil creatures thrive in it, using its inky blackness for their own twisted purposes. Impenetrable at its worst and merely dim at its best. Feeding the fuel for one's worst nightmares.

Darkness fears nothing, except for the light. As far as anyone can remember, the light has always fought against the dark. Its battle is one, which has continued in silence since the beginning of the world. A struggle taken for granted by those who have witnessed the day and night. The night is no match for the sun, causing the blackness to stay away for hours at a time. The moon and stars with their pale glow can break the eerie silence that seems to follow it all around. A glowing fire with its licking flames, dances merrily this way and that, warning the darkness off. The fire flaunts openly, the darkness cannot take hold of it or even threaten it. Even the firefly so tiny and frail, can scare the weight of it away with its warm glow.

The evil living within the depths of darkness also fears the light. Its shining rays blind their eyes and weakens the heart of those who love the night. They hate all that light stands for and those who rely on it to keep fear at bay. It is only the strongest who learns to use light to defeat the dark and everything that lives within it.

Chapter One

Galena sat quietly regarding the campfire dancing merrily before her. Visions from the cave still racing through her mind, causing her to cringe with each one. She turned to look at Elenio's sleeping face, envying him for the peace he seemed to have. She'd tried lying down, but the nightmares began and she found herself sitting up, drenched in sweat, her own screams still ringing in her ears. A lifetime would not be long enough to forget what her mind made real.

Mira warned her before she'd reached the cave what she could expect once she crossed the mouth, but even then, Galena hadn't been fully prepared. She didn't understand what she truly feared. The cave almost broke her. It pushed her to the very brink of madness and was about to give a final shove, causing her to enter into a void she would not have been able to return from, when Elenio saved her. Through the mental link they shared as commitment partners, he pushed her forward. Even when she begged for death to take her, he'd been there, encouraging her, pushing her harder than even the magic of the cave could have. It was only with his mind linked to hers, unable to see the horrors she beheld, was she able to find the Sword of Lumina and return to the reality of the world to which she'd been born into.

She rather hoped that once she left the confines of the cavern walls, her memories of the place would dissolve just as the bodies within did, but it wasn't so. Unlike the stories she heard from elves who'd crossed the path of the cave and the guardian, she remembered everything in detail. Elenio hadn't forgotten either and they both attributed this to the successful retrieval of the famed sword.

Galena shivered more from memories than the cold. She slipped from their bed and sat by the fire, savoring its warmth and light. She pulled the sword from its shabby scabbard and regarded it carefully. It looked battered and worn, much like the swords hidden beneath her childhood home used for thousands of years. However, as far as Galena knew, this couldn't be true. She'd never heard of the Sword of Lumina being used in any great battle or any battle at all. Returning the blade to the scabbard and placing both by her pack, she wrapped her arms around her legs and continued to stare at the fire, the images of dead loved ones floating in the smoke that curled and drifted in the air above the bright flames.

Galena sighed deeply, shaking her head to clear her mind of its morbid thoughts. She knew, with no uncertainty, Mira was right on several accounts. However, one thing struck her more powerfully than the rest. The whole experience taught her what her greatest fear was and made her stronger for it. She knew she would never again watch a loved one die, not while she still had breath in her body and magic flowing through her veins. They would have to kill her first if they ever wanted to touch her family, of that she was sure.

Standing, she looked at Elenio, sleeping peacefully and surrounded by a mound of blankets from their packs. She smiled as she looked at him, her heart clinching painfully as she watched. When she'd first emerged from the hated cave Mira created, he looked shocked at her appearance. It appeared she'd been through a terrible battle, even though in her mind, she'd experienced something far worse than any battle she'd ever fought. Then relief flooded through the features on his face and she could feel them radiate through his mind as well. All she could think was that here he stood, alive and well for the most part, a fact she would never allow to change. He raced across the clearing and embraced her for the longest time until Twoit bit him rather harder than necessary on the leg, causing him to let go.

She had stood back and watched him practice a few choice words while scratching Twoit's head until she too calmed down. Healing Elenio's bite quickly and the other cuts and bruises he suffered as a result of wrestling with vines intent on keeping him from the cave, they decided to head out immediately. Neither of them wanted to stay

3

anywhere near the guardian or the cursed cave. As far as Galena was concerned, if she ever came to the Western woods again, it would be too soon.

Once they stopped, Galena changed into her spare outfit and true to her word burned the clothing still covered with the blood from the bodies of her loved ones. She caused a heavy rain shower to fall on them, washing away the remains of her imagination from her face, hands, and hair. She hadn't wanted to stop for a bath and that had been the quickest way for her to feel clean again, although the smell of death still lingered.

Sitting back down by the fireside, Galena closed her eyes, resting her head on her raised knees. She was tired. They'd been traveling for almost a week and during that time she'd only managed to sneak in a couple of hours of sleep. Those precious hours were riddled with nightmares. Haunting images of her family dying one after the other in the cave with Galena standing helplessly by as she watched their demise.

Taking a deep breath, Galena focused her thoughts on Elenio. He'd been extremely supportive ever since she had emerged from the cave. He never once asked her what she had seen, for which she was deeply grateful. She would never be able to put to words the horror her own mind had had in store for her. She realized he'd seen some of what she had, but it had not affected him the same way. He hadn't held the body, felt the warm blood soaking into his clothes, and heard the death rattle of a last breath. He only experienced briefly, what she had been unable to escape on her own.

He wore a knowing look every time he glanced at her, making Galena more certain that to an extent, he had been there through part of the ordeal, otherwise she never would have made it through. It had been Elenio pushing her on mentally that kept her going when she wanted to lie down and die. However, she also knew in order for him to have survived what she went through, he had to have shielded himself from the full emotional scale of what she suffered. Galena realized she'd lost part of herself in that horrible cave, a part she was unsure she would ever get back. *Why couldn't it have taken the memories with it,* she thought glumly to herself.

"Because it made you stronger and it will continue to make you stronger." Galena jerked her head up and fell back all in one motion. She found herself looking up into the face of Mira, smiling sadly down at her. Anger and sorrow welled up in her as she looked at the beloved goddess. She could have been more honest with her. She could have told her exactly what she was going up against in the cave, but instead she had been vague, telling her the bare minimum.

"Now you choose to show yourself," Galena said bitterly.

"Do not be angry with me, child. I could not tell you what I did not know. Only you know your own mind."

Galena snorted in unbelief as she turned her head like a sulking child.

"Galena, I gave you all the tools that I could to help you survive. I told you the journey through would be more difficult than anything else you encountered. Did I lie?"

Mira's voice was harsher than Galena could ever remember it being and unwillingly, she felt the tears spring into her eyes, feelings of shame at her words filling her. "You did. I just didn't realize how hard it would be and still continues to be," Galena said as she wiped the traitorous tears from her eyes. She was determined she would never cry again after her experience. She felt warm, soft fingers lifting her chin up so she was looking Mira in the eye.

"Because you have faced your own fear, there is nothing that will stand in your way now. You have defeated my greatest challenge and have the means to defeat Rau, not only with a weapon of light, but with a stronger heart and mind. I told you that you could not face the fears of Tomiro until you faced the fears that would consume your own mind and you have. You are now ready for the last battle, our last chance at freedom."

Mira held Galena's eyes, making her feel as if she were staring into her very soul. Her bright, green eyes held centuries within them and a peace Galena so longed for. She felt the tightness in her chest loosen and the parts of her mind and heart begin to heal. The memories were still there, but the bite that normally went with them was beginning to fade. Her breathing eased and the same peace she saw in Mira's eyes spilled over her in wonderful waves. She experienced a weariness that only comes with a hard ordeal and sleepless nights wash over her. As they did, she felt herself falling back and drifting into a dreamless sleep.

Galena awoke to sunlight streaming in through the bare branches of the trees surrounding her. She sat up quickly and realized she was in the bed she made the night before. Elenio glanced at her from the side of the campfire and seeing she was awake resumed eating the loaf of bread he'd started. Galena blinked and tried to recall exactly how she ended up in the bed when she distinctly remembered sitting by the fire talking with Mira when she had drifted off. Try as she might, she was unable to think how she managed such a feat.

"I saw you sleeping on the ground sometime last night and brought you back to bed. You didn't even stir," Elenio answered her unspoken question through a mouthful of bread.

"How long have I been sleeping?" Galena asked as she stifled a yawn.

"Through most of the day. I couldn't bear to wake you when I know you've had so little sleep the last several nights." He stuffed the last piece of bread in his mouth and dusted off his hands before he stood. "Do you want me to get something for you to eat or will you grace us with your presence today?" he asked grinningly wickedly as he bowed low, his gaze never leaving her face.

She needed something to throw, but found nothing that would do damage within reach. Getting up with as much dignity as possible, she walked over to her pack and retrieved some of the food at the very bottom. She found a few crumbs of what looked like sweet bread and some minute pieces of cheese. Taking a brief moment to make more of the food so she wouldn't completely deplete their supplies, she sat down next to the fire. She hadn't put up the protective barriers for the last couple of nights because she knew Rau had called all things dark to Blackwell in preparation for the coming war, but now with the chill of evening settling around her, she regretted it. Taking a moment, she quickly set up the air hut and ring of fire, instantly feeling a difference in the temperature around her. *Nice and cozy*, she thought dryly.

"Sure, when you're cold, you create an instant change in temperature. Don't mind that I've been cold for a while."

"Well, I am more important. Besides, you could have stirred the fire," she said saucily to him, taking a bite of cheese as she did so. It was the first time in days she felt properly hungry. Elenio chucked a piece of wood at her for which she waved a hand carelessly, blowing it off course with the wind that she directed.

"Well, that wasn't fair," Elenio said, brows furrowed in disappointment.

Galena just grinned in response. She made quick work of her meal, taking care to leave enough to make more with later and shoved those pieces in her pack before she stood, brushing her backside off as she did.

"Feel like going a couple of rounds with me. I need to burn some energy if I'm going to sleep more tonight."

"Had a good rest then?" Elenio asked, curiosity and happiness written all over his face and in his thoughts.

"A dreamless one," Galena said, shrugging nonchalantly as she bent down to retrieve her sword. She hadn't fought with it before and was worried that it would handle differently than her old blade. When she picked it up though, it felt natural in her hand, like an extension of her arm, which is what she had always learned a proper sword should feel like.

Twirling the blade around her and getting into her starting stance, she waited for Elenio to retrieve his own blade, smiling as he bumbled along. He grabbed his sword and striding over to her, he prepared in his own way. Not giving him a chance to land the first blow, Galena came at him immediately. Within two strokes, she found her blade at his throat while he eyed her strangely. Stepping back, she prepared to go again, only this time, waiting for him to begin their session. He came at her, moving quicker than she ever saw him move, but once again, she had him on the ground within a couple of moves, her sword pointing at his chest.

"Okay, you're normally very difficult to beat, but you have a whole new level of quickness you didn't have before and I'm guessing it has to do with your new blade," he said, sitting up as Galena backed away once more. "I'm not going to be able to get the better of you no matter how many times we go around unless I have several elves helping me."

Galena looked at the sword with new respect in her eyes. She knew the sword gave her a greater awareness of everything around her, a clearer way of thinking, but more energy as well. She noticed this as soon as she touched it in the cave. Elenio even told her she seemed to glow with a subtle light ever since she left the entrance of the cave. Apparently, there was more to this sword than she had originally gave it credit. She looked at the sword in her hand, wondering what other surprises she had in store as the owner of this infamous blade.

Chapter Two

Tark watched his generals work with the different groups they'd chosen for the purpose of training as many elves as possible in the shortest amount of time. Granted, Mira sped up this process considerably, but Tark still felt it was necessary his lead elves teach several groups just as he taught them. This allowed them to train many more elves than it would have been possible for just him alone. He still worked with his top ten chosen on a daily basis to keep up their skills, but they spent most of their time now helping to prepare others for the upcoming war against Rau.

Among the other elves was his commitment partner, Taura. He placed her in Morgo's group because Morgo had become one of his most trusted advisors and generals as well as an excellent teacher. Tark wanted to make sure he gave Taura every chance to become the best possible warrior she could. He hadn't been crazy about the idea of her joining in the war with hundreds of other elves, but after their argument, he relented. Now, not only did she train with Morgo most mornings and evenings, but also with Tark any free moment he could spare. He knew Morgo was a very able teacher. Even so, Tark felt it was his training that pushed Taura the hardest and made her the capable fighter she was becoming.

While Taura was busy training and dealing with every other aspect of being the leader of a small army, their daughter, Silva, spent most of her time with Quona, Amrick's daughter. Amrick was the main leader of the village the elves claimed as their training site, as well as Silva's guardian should anything happen to him or Taura. She'd opted out of being trained for the sole reason that the remaining elves would need a

9

capable leader and she felt she was just the elf for the job. She was strong, able and decisive when the moment called for it. She didn't back down from a challenge, and the only time Tark ever saw fear in her was the time she thought she had lost Quona to some torlics.

Before Tark would even agree to training Taura, they made sure Silva would be taken care of by a capable elf. They both considered Venia for a short moment before deciding, due to her mental state, they would have to find someone else to take care of her and her infant son as well. With the death of her husband, Melan, Venia had been stricken. She was mentally broken, much to Tark and Taura's dismay. She was barely able to take care of herself. However, since her arrival at Corista, she had made some progress. Such as starting to feed herself and acknowledging others by staring vacantly at them. Although taking care of her infant son and grooming herself was completely out of the question.

After ruling out Venia, that left only one other elf in their mind who could raise their daughter well. They approached Amrick with the request of being Silva's guardian to which she graciously agreed. They approached Morgo with the request of caring for Venia if they were unable to return and if nothing happened to him during battle, as he had taken a particular interest in her since the moment of their meeting. He took in her vacant expression and her lack of participation in daily activities or anything surrounding her with great interest. On the second day of their arrival, Taura found him patiently setting food before her and talking soothingly to her all the while. He held her young son, Jamin, on his hip like an experienced father. Other times, he could been seen leading her around the village and pointing out things that interested him or just reading to her while she stared blankly at different objects in the room. When Taura told Tark this, he'd been amused and approached Morgo. Morgo simply stated he found Venia interesting and left it at that. Tark however, suspected there was more to it.

Almost a week went by when they began to notice small changes in Venia's demeanor because of her time with Morgo. Life would flicker in her eyes and dance around her mouth for a few short moments before fleeing her once more. She showed signs of noticing Jamin when her son became upset or laughed. Taura even found Venia staring at the washbasin, as if she was waiting to be bathed. They were small victories, and Tark couldn't help but see them as good omens.

Tark focused once more on the mock sparring occurring all around him and smiled with satisfaction. He noticed a group of elves collecting in the center of the training field and wandered over to see what was causing all the commotion. In the center of the group of elves, he found Naradin going against Hasa and Weila in a practice battle. He smiled, thinking Naradin didn't stand a chance against the terrible two. The twins were incredibly fast and although Naradin had a great knack for staying calm in the midst of fighting, he still couldn't compete against their speed. However, he lasted a great deal longer than Tark would have ever thought he would. It was several minutes later and to a great roar of cheering from the watching crowd, Naradin pinned Hasa, but found himself at the mercy of Weila, who had a knife at his throat. Tark clapped with the rest of the crowd. It was a great effort on Naradin's part.

Tark had met with his closest elves, the ones he considered his ten generals that morning on the progress with the different groups they selected and worked with on a daily basis. They too, were extremely proud of how far all the elves in each of their groups had come in the short amount of time. They hadn't known as he did, that Mira was at work in the elves' training. He felt it was an unnecessary piece of knowledge and decided to let them take the credit for the incredible progress. He figured this would do wonders for their self-esteem.

Hasa and Weila decided to train groups together due to their uncanny ability of working as a team. They had been very successful in this particular area. Morgo and Nina had been working with the underground elves on honing their magical abilities during battles and using their powers to aide others during combat. They both reported the few underground elves who chose to fight, had come a long way. They were able to increase the amount of magic they were able to do, without passing out.

Before leaving the underground world, most of these elves only used magic for day-to-day use and were unaccustomed to using it for any other purposes. The first week alone, caused most of them to remain unconscious off and on for hours at a time. Now, only one or two would overdo it, causing them to lose consciousness for a short time instead of the hours that would have been normal before. The other generals were also reporting the same improvements, much to Tark's delight.

It was nearing noon and Tark was starving, but he had to head toward Amrick's house first. He had received a message that some of the scouts he sent out were coming back with reports earlier that morning, but he hadn't had a chance to head there until now. They were waiting for him at Amrick's until he had a chance to discuss the happenings in Tomiro. Tark was pleased to be heading there because he hadn't been able to see his daughter yet that day and he missed her dearly. He was called away for an urgent matter long before she awoke and then stayed busy for the remainder of the time.

Tark strode into Amrick's front yard, smiling as his tiny daughter and Quona came into view. They both wielded sticks, practicing their own form of sparring, before ending in a fit of giggles at each other's attempts to disarm the other.

"Keep that up and I'll have to recruit both of you for the coming war," Tark said with humor in his voice.

Silva spun around, squealing with delight as she took off at a full sprint toward her father. Tark braced himself before stretching his arms out wide in preparation to catch the flying spitfire known as his daughter. Taking one last step and propelling herself forward, she sprung into his arms, wrapping her own little limbs tightly around his neck.

"I missed you this morning, Daddy," she said quietly into his ear.

"I missed you too, little one." He hugged her tightly and kissed the top of her head. "Do you want to come in with me while I talk to the scouts I sent out?"

Silva shook her head as she answered, "Amrick told us we needed to stay outdoors while you talked with the elves. She said we could come back in when it was time for our noonday meal."

Tark pulled back, evaluating Silva's serious expression while the feeling of his stomach dropping filled the rest of his senses. It always made him nervous to discuss with others the whereabouts of Rau or any of his soldiers. Now, with the knowledge Amrick didn't want the little ones to overhear what the scouts had to say, did not bode well at all.

"Well, run along then and I'll see you in a few minutes," he told her as he set her down, his voice sounding falsely cheery in his own ears.

Silva kissed him on his cheek before running toward Quona. The smile he wore just moments before, slipped from his face as he walked up to Amrick's front door, opened it, then stepped through. What he saw confirmed his fears. The news he was about to hear was not going to be good. So much for hoping Rau would have a change of heart, deciding he'd had enough ruling and was going to join the elf ranks. Tark sighed heavily and then sat at one of the chairs surrounding their eating table. "Let me have it. What has caused all the gloomy faces?"

* * * *

Tark raced toward the training fields. He had to gather his generals, especially Morgo and Nina. They needed answers, the ones only magical elves could give with the mirror waters. Not waiting until he had the attention of everyone's watchful eyes, he raced to the center of the field before shouting as loudly as he could, "Generals, to my home now!" He sprinted toward his tree home, pleased to note his generals caught his urgency and ran along at the same pace as he did. Morgo reached his doorstep at the same time as Tark breathing heavily too. "We need your mirror waters and Nina's as well. I want to see a couple different things and as quickly as possible."

Morgo nodded briefly before running up the stairs to retrieve his and Nina's mirror water bowls. The remaining nine raced into the room and Tark indicated they needed to find a seat while they waited for Morgo's return. The look of concern was pasted on everyone's face as they regarded Tark and fought to catch their breath. He returned their looks, indicating with a single finger they had to wait until they were all together to hear the news. Morgo returned shortly, holding two wooden bowls in his hand. Reaching the last step, he walked quickly toward Nina, handing her a bowl before sitting down next to her. He looked up expectantly toward Tark, trying quietly to catch his breath.

"I have just met with the scouts. I know this may come as a surprise to you," he started, sarcasm thick in his voice, "but Rau has sent a small army toward us."

Morgo held Tark's gaze, but many of the others looked away, staring at their hands or the floor in an uncomfortable silence.

"The scouts reported several thousand of Rau's soldiers, no more than a week out from here, traveling at an incredible pace. Morgo, can you bring up an image of the army heading our way? Nina, I need you to see if Galena will appear in the waters this time." The last couple of times he asked to see Galena, they were unable to view anything. Tark attributed this malfunction to the fact Galena may have been in the cave at the time. However, it had been a week since he requested an image of her, so he was hoping they would be able to see something this time.

The group leaned over Morgo's bowl first and gasped at what they saw. There were at least twice as many dark creatures as there were elves, trained and ready to fight. They saw everything from torlics to the giant earagos. Instead of his heart dropping into the pit of his stomach, he felt as if his heart lodged itself in his throat making it difficult to breath.

"Dear gods, what have we gotten ourselves into?" he heard Yeia mutter somewhere to his left.

"I'd say we're in for quite the battle," Fala said with more calm than Tark felt.

His insides squirmed and quaked with a fear that threatened to show itself, making his generals realize what a coward he truly was. He took a calming breath before addressing Morgo again. "Can you show us Blackwell?"

Morgo nodded before furrowing his brow in concentration. Before them appeared another image, every bit as disturbing as the one that it replaced. Thousands more dark and disturbing creatures filled the image in the bowl as they shifted and moved around the great black castle. Tark heard Hasa groan behind him as she beheld the image captivating them all.

"And here I was hoping he sent the majority our way in order to cut us off before we even got started," Tark said dryly. He put his head in his hands, praying silently to Mira for a peace he did not feel, but desperately needed. "Nina, do you have anything?" he heard himself whispering, dreading the answer.

"Yes."

Tark jerked his head up, relief so profound and comforting, stealing over him as he stepped over to peer into Nina's bowl. Galena appeared to be walking through a forest, a new blade hung at her waist. If this was the Sword of Lumina, it was nothing like Tark imagined. Instead of being adorned with jewels and wealth that none of them had ever experienced, it was held in a shabby and worn looking scabbard. The hilt covered in a worn looking leather. Nothing fancy at all. Tark's brows furrowed, questions racing through him faster than he could keep track of. Shaking his head, he returned his focus to the problem at hand. Galena looked well, other than a tightness around her eyes and a glow that had not been there before she left. "She survived," he whispered mainly to himself.

A collective sigh left the mouths of several of his generals.

"We need to get prepared. We cannot let them get as far as the village. We need to go to them so we give our loved ones as much of a chance at life as possible. We'll send out Morak and some of his elves to pick off as many creatures as he can, while the rest of the army moves out."

Morak jerked his head once in agreement, as he continued to stare at the image still on display in Morgo's bowl. Morak had been training his own group of elves in the art of shooting a bow and arrow as this was his strength. "It won't be much, but we'll do what we can from a distance," Morak said calmly.

"Stay as far away as you can. Don't get in a direct battle until we have all collected and made ready to fight. We're already severely outnumbered so let's not make that gap even wider. However, I want you to cause as much damage as possible," Tark said, not taking his eyes off Galena. "The rest of us need to get prepared to head out in the morning. Morgo, tell Pangoro what to look for once we're gone so he'll know when to give the villagers the heads up on when to leave. The rest of you spread the word. We leave for battle tomorrow morning at sunrise."

Chapter Three

Galena stared across the fire at Elenio. The heartache she associated every time she looked at him, faded to almost nothing thanks to Mira. She had been able to sleep peacefully the last couple of nights without any dreams at all. Galena counted this as a blessing, and smiled as she continued to watch Elenio eat his sweet bread with great enthusiasm.

"Hungry?" she asked, smirking at him while she chewed on a grape.

"That's a minor understatement. If you hadn't stopped when you did, I might have resorted to knocking you out with a big branch so I could eat," he said winking an eye at her.

She smiled and shifted her gaze to the fire, fighting an image from the cave that came to mind.

"I know what you're going through," she heard Elenio say quietly.

She looked up to see Elenio staring at her, empathy written clearly on his face along with the haunted look she associated with the time she nearly killed herself using magic.

"I watched you die too. True, I didn't think I would have to wait long before I joined you, so it wasn't as painful, but I knew you'd left me." He threw a small twig into the fire before he continued. "If I hadn't had a mission, the thought that the healing waters at Mira's View would save you, I don't know what I would have done. I probably would have found a way to join you in the Land of the Gods."

Galena nodded. The image of a dying Elenio swam before her eyes. She knew how close she'd come to taking her own life. Sadness swept over her as Elenio saw what she saw in his own mind.

"I wanted to die," she choked. "If you hadn't been in my head, I would have killed myself. I was coming very close to that point, but I heard you somewhere in the back of my mind."

"I know. I felt it too. I couldn't let my thoughts stay completely with you because of what you felt. Just peeking in from time to time almost destroyed me. Being commitment partners is so much deeper than just being in love. You truly feel like part of me and without that part, I couldn't imagine going on," he whispered. Standing up, he walked around the fire and sat behind her, putting his arms around her shoulders, and resting his chin on her head. "It's over and I think we have both learned an important lesson."

"Oh yeah? What's that?" Galena asked, smiling as she placed her own hands on top of Elenio's.

"My death was more devastating than yours."

Galena shook her head as she elbowed Elenio in the side, causing him to chuckle. "You're impossible."

"And you love me, so what does that say about you?"

"That I have bigger issues than anyone realized."

Elenio kissed the back of her head before squeezing her briefly. "No matter what, we stay together. We're stronger together and I don't ever want you out of my sight again. Time will ease the memories and the pain. You'll see," he whispered in her ear.

"Mira came to me a couple of nights ago. She gave me the gift of that time and took away my dreams. The memories are still there, but I can handle them now. That hasn't changed my resolve though. I will never watch one of my own perish again. Not while I have life to stop it." Galena gritted her teeth, the determination that she felt apparent in the hardness of her voice.

"Just make sure to take care of you as well. If you go, I will follow." Elenio buried his face in her hair.

Galena turned her face so that she was looking at Elenio and kissed him gently. "I'll do my best," she whispered with a ghost of a smile on her face.

"How far do you think we have before we get back to the village?" Elenio asked, changing the subject abruptly.

"We've been traveling for about a week, so I would say about a week or two more. If we don't have to stop at any villages like the last time, it may be quicker."

Twoit came over and climbed onto Galena's lap before curling up into a ball. She rested her head on her paws, closed her eyes, and fell asleep. Galena scratched the ferret's head while she watched the fire.

"We'll make it in time," Elenio said, answering the question still floating around in her mind.

She smiled at his reassurance, but didn't feel comforted by it, as he seemed to be.

"Let's get to sleep so we can get an earlier start."

Yawning at the thought of sleep, Galena nodded her head before quickly creating a tree bed, complete with a leaf layer for comfort. The thought of sleep no longer teased her, but called to her gently with promises of rest and renewal.

Elenio stood and offering a hand, which Galena took, pulled her to her feet. She stretched and took in her surroundings, before heading to bed where Elenio was already lying and pulling a blanket over himself. She looked up through the trees and found the stars above winking down at her with the ability to ward away the night and the evil things that hid there. She climbed into bed, pulling the blankets over her as she did. As soon as her head hit the leaves, she drifted off into a world without dreams.

Galena opened her eyes to find herself in the middle of nowhere and nothing. She noticed a dim light and found the source of it immediately. Galena was startled to see Mira, once surrounded by blinding, white light was a mere shadow of her former glory. She seemed to flicker in and out of Galena's vision. The more Galena tried to focus, the worse the flickering became. She found that if she focused on the area around Mira, the goddess's image stayed put a little better.

"What has happened to you?" Galena asked in horror at the goddess's fallen state.

"Haulua grows stronger every hour. His rage has consumed him and given him more power than any of us realized. My brothers and I grow weak with our fight," the goddess answered in a voice full of weariness.

"But you were just fine a couple of days ago," Galena nearly shouted, panic filling her.

"Weeks, days, hours, and minutes, they are all the same to the gods. Time is different for us. I don't have long for visits such as these. It wears on me further and I need all my strength to contain Haulua. You must hurry for the war is beginning. Rau has sent an army to put a stop to your brother and the elves he has trained. If they are to succeed in the end, you will have to be a part of the battles. Do not stop other than to rest, for your timing will almost be too short. Travel southeast and you will find them here."

Galena saw in her mind's eye a picture of a small valley covered in the dead grass of a retreating winter. On the nearest side, were the elves and their camp. The dark creatures consumed the far side. She knew the area, for they had traveled through it on their way to the Western woods. It was a few days journey from the village of Corista, where Tark stayed behind.

"Why have they stayed so close to the village?" Galena asked, horrified at the thought of all those dark creatures overtaking the village Tark now called home.

"That was all the further they got before they ran into Rau's forces. He instructed them to go at a fast pace and because of the marks on their own foreheads; the dark creatures had no choice, but to obey."

At this point, Mira began flickering so badly Galena felt sick from watching her. "You must hurry my child." Mira flickered once more before she faded completely, leaving Galena feeling disturbed at best. How much time did they have?

* * * *

Tark rolled the map out further, placing small stones at each of the corners to examine it more closely. Morak indicated the entire southern half of the valley was covered in dark creatures with the earagos at the front. Morak's small party picked off several smaller groups within Rau's army, but that still left thousands of creatures to deal with. The sheer number of torlics, narooks, and other creatures Tark hadn't even laid eyes on, let alone knew the names of, made Tark sweat profusely.

Where are you, Galena, he asked himself as he did every time he thought of what they were up against. He was bending over to see where he could sneak in more small units to do damage within the enemy's camp, when Taura came up behind him. He felt her concern and fear as she placed her hands on his shoulders. She massaged the tired muscles of his neck and shoulders, causing a sigh to escape his lips as he leaned his head back. He closed his eyes and enjoyed his commitment partner's onslaught against the fatigue and stress that had taken up residence in his body. Kissing the top of his head, she walked around to the other side of the table he'd set up in their tent and sat down with a flop. Sighing deeply, she propped her elbow on the armrest and placed her head on her hand as she regarded Tark.

"I take it your meeting did not go well?"

"It went as well as could be expected, all things considered. Morak says between him and his soldiers, they have dispersed of a hundred or more torlics and narooks. Although an earagos noticed them. They had to flee back to safety with the giant brute hot on their heels. Morak said the giant didn't even try to chase them past the river, it just stood on its side of the bank and laughed at them." Tark pinched the bridge of his nose, tiredness consuming him as he did so.

"You need to rest or you will be worthless to us," Taura said gently.

"How can I rest when I feel like I have led all these elves to their death and with no sign of Galena yet? You do realize they outnumber us ten to one."

Since arriving, Tark discovered the scouts' original reports of being outnumbered two to one were grossly inaccurate. He had an army of roughly five hundred. Rau's army numbered closer to five thousand. The scary part, in Tark's mind, was this was less than half of Rau's total forces. The rest of his men stayed behind at Blackwell should Tark accomplish the impossible. *Definitely, overkill,* Tark thought dryly.

"You still need rest," Taura said reasonably.

Tark looked at Taura, feeling annoyed, but realizing she was right.

"Morgo can manage anything urgent while you rest."

"Wake me…"

"I'll wake you if anything important comes up or if anything changes. Now, get some sleep." She stood, rolling up the maps and tucked them up under her arm. Walking over to Tark and tilting his face so she was looking directly into his eyes, whispered, "I love you. Sleep well." Taura kissed him softly and walked out of the tent, closing the flap behind her.

He stared for some time at the inside of the tent, reminiscing how his life had been just a year ago. If anyone had told him he would be leading a small army into a battle against Rau, he would have laughed and sent them off to a healer. Now as it was, he was unsure of himself and desperate for Galena's return.

He awoke with a jarring crash when his chair had tipped over, spilling him unceremoniously to the floor. Tark looked around, startled and unsure of where he was. It took a moment for him to remember he was no longer in his comfortable tree house, but inside a large tent. Apparently, more tired than even he realized, if falling asleep while in mid thought wasn't a problem. Shaking his head wearily, he slowly stood, stretching his arms and legs in the process. He rubbed his eyes and walked over to his bed.

The magic elves decided, reasonably, that creating tree homes for everyone right at the edge of the battlefield would be a poor use of their power and it would be best if their energy were put to use on defenses and preparing their weapons for battle. However, they created the large tents and hammocks for the entire army, using materials they brought and prepared specially in the village prior to coming here. It proved convenient and useful when an entire camp with room enough for everyone was constructed in a couple of hours. The underground elves had come a long way in a short amount of time.

Tark sat wearily at the edge of his hammock. It had taken him several attempts to be able to sit on the blasted material without being dumped on the ground in an undignified pile. Indeed, the first time he tried it, he found himself flying backward and conking the back of his head so hard on the ground, he saw stars. He remembered it had been quite some time for Taura to quit laughing before she was able to ask if he was alright and then to retrieve Morgo when he had trouble responding. He was getting to be as bad as Galena. He managed to get his shoes off before flopping back onto the hammock where he fell asleep almost instantly.

Tark rolled over to his side, and bumped into Taura. Lifting his head slightly, he looked around and saw it was now night. Feeling slightly alarmed, he sat up waking Taura in the process.

"Lie back down. We have posted guards and they will be replaced every hour. There is nothing you can do right now. Nothing has happened and no one needs your immediate attention, so go back to sleep." She rolled over facing away from him before resuming her own slumber.

Tark looked at her, watching the slow rise and fall of her shoulder, knowing it was unlikely she would remember telling him any of this. Smiling and settling back down, he closed his eyes and felt himself begin to drift off once more when he heard a faint voice somewhere in the back of his mind. Tark strained to hear it as it faded. The words came together in his mind and he struggled to make sense of them until finally, it clicked.

She comes. Prepare yourself for the battle is about to begin.

Feeling extremely unsettled with the prospect of fighting the next day, for he was sure that was what Mira meant; he rolled over and wrapped a protective arm around Taura before drifting off into a fitful slumber.

* * * *

Galena sat up with the first rays of light shining on her face. Flipping her blankets back, she swung her legs over the edge of the bed and lowering herself to the ground, grabbed a bowl from her pack, and filled it with water. Thinking of Tark, she saw him surrounded by different elves, among them were Fala, Morgo, Morak, Nina, Taura, and several others she did not recognize. It looked like they were inside a large tent, which made sense considering what Mira told her the night before. The army of elves would have surely left the village and were now on their way to the battle for which Galena must be present at if they were to come out victorious.

Putting down the bowl, Galena reached for her pack and created several loaves of bread, cheese, and some fruit. Most of it she put back in their packs, but left out a couple small loaves for their morning meal.

Shaking Elenio awake before she pulled off the blankets to pack as well, she tossed him a loaf of bread, which he barely caught.

"What's the rush?" he asked before yawning widely.

"The battle is about to begin. Tark has already started toward the army Rau sent out." She shoved the blankets into their packs, and grabbing Twoit around the middle, placed the tiny ferret on top of her blanket, and flipped the flap over.

Elenio sat up, looking alarmed. "How did you find that out?"

"Mira told me in a vision and then I checked in the mirror waters." Galena strapped the Sword of Lumina to her waist. Bending over, she retrieved Elenio's blade and tossed it to him. He caught it with more success than the bread and quickly prepared himself to go as well. "I hope you slept well because we have a great deal of ground we need to cover today." Galena looked grimly at Elenio who returned the look, biting off a chunk of bread as he did so. Sweeping his arm in a wide manner, he bowed his head, indicating he expected her to lead the way.

They alternated between walking and running through the entire day and into the night. Never stopping as Mira suggested. Galena told Elenio of her latest encounter with Mira, and found he was just as disturbed by the goddess's appearance or lack of appearance as she had been earlier. The urgency she felt was catching and Elenio pushed on as well, both hesitant to even stop late in the night to sleep for a couple of hours.

"We have to or we're not going to get very far tomorrow. If I remember correctly, we still have a couple days ahead of us until we reach the valley Mira indicated they would be."

"I know. I just hate the thought of Tark going into battle without us, or I should say without me. I still have some revenge I'd like to take out on those great hulking beasts for the strangle hold they put on me," Elenio said, a faraway look on his face.

"I already took care of those," Galena said smirking. She put the protective barriers around them while creating a bed for them.

"Well, we can't all be hugely powerful so I'll have to take my revenge on the ones I come across and pretend they're the same ones."

Galena rolled her eyes at this statement. She bit off a piece of cheese and climbed into the bed, not even bothering with a blanket. The days were starting to get warmer. With the ring of fire and air hut, it was almost too warm. Elenio climbed in beside her and wrapped his arms around her, pulling her close to him. Galena threw an arm around his waist after she stuffed the rest of her cheese in her mouth. She chewed quietly, listening to the sound of Elenio's breath becoming slow and regular, assuring her he'd fallen asleep. The words of Mira rang through her mind as she too drifted into slumber.

Much sooner than she would have normally arose, Galena sat up, the urgency she felt the day before increased tenfold. She assumed this was a feeling sent from Mira because it served as a convenient wake up call. Judging by the dim light surrounding them, it was just before dawn.

Shaking Elenio gently until he began to stir, she once again made ready for their long journey. *If we can keep the same pace as we did yesterday, we might make it to the battle on time,* Galena thought.

She heard Elenio groan as he rolled over and sat up. Swinging his legs over the edge, he stretched his arms high into the air while yawning widely. Galena watched him grimace when he stood.

"Oh, I'm stiff," he moaned more to himself. He continued to stretch his legs and arms, bending this way and that in order to stretch the tired muscles in his back.

Galena thought of the muscles repairing themselves from running the day before and quickened up the pace of it, so relief replaced the grimace Elenio wore just moments before. She did the same to her own muscles, the same relief buzzed through her own body.

"Are you up to getting energized again?" Galena asked while she packed their belongings.

"Are you kidding? With the workout we had yesterday and the two hours of sleep last night, I wasn't sure how far we would make it today. I think that's a great idea."

Nodding in agreement, Galena thought of life giving energy flowing into their blood. Instantly, she felt more alive, her senses were more alert. The blue sky looked brighter and the trees surrounding them were richer brown. She took a deep breath and noticed even the air smelled sweeter. Galena felt she could run for hours, days, or even weeks. Looking at Elenio, she saw the same alert expression on his face.

He smiled at her and reaching down to grab his sword and scabbard, strapped them around his waist as Galena collected the rest of their things.

"Remember this won't last forever, so we need to be someplace safe when we come down from the energy burst." Galena looked around and seeing the direction of the sun, headed off at an incredible sprint with Elenio on her heels.

That day and the majority of the night, they covered twice as much ground as they had the day before. Galena believed she could go on running through the night and the next day, but Elenio proved to be the voice of reason on this matter.

"We could, but the crash that's going to follow this huge burst of energy will be even harder on our bodies. We have to rest for a least a short while and get something to eat," he responded to her unspoken thoughts.

Galena was annoyed, but agreed, knowing he was right. Grabbing Twoit from her pack, she put the ferret on the ground. She noticed the ferret was still half-asleep so she proceeded to get the food and campfire ready.

Elenio grabbed a couple pieces of fruit from his own pack, tossing an apple to Galena, which she nearly missed because she hadn't been paying attention.

"Hey, next time warn me," she said grouchily at him.

To which he tossed another apple at her, succeeding in smacking her in the back of the head. She turned to glare at him and found him smiling broadly down at her.

"Ooops."

"Ooops this," she said under breath. Standing quickly, she flung her hand in the air, directing the wind up and under Elenio, and raising him high into the air. She directed the air toward a tree, noting the reaction Elenio had by covering his face with his arms, and yelling for her to put him down all the while. Instead of slamming him into the tree as he obviously thought she was about to do, she made the wind deposit him on the highest branch that would support his weight. Keeping the wind there and ready in case he should lose his balance, she looked up at him and returned his previous smile with a wide one of her own. "Have fun getting down." She turned and walked back to the campfire, retrieved the apple he had hit her in the head with, and took a giant bite before sitting down to watch Elenio's slow progress climbing out of the tree.

After a short while, Galena gave in to Elenio's grumblings when he got half way down from his previous position. She sent a gust of wind to help him the rest of the way to the ground. She had the wind drop him on his butt though, making her feel better about giving in and helping him in the first place.

"You used to be a lot more fun before you used magic for everything," he said, still wearing a sour expression on his face.

"Like I said before, a lot more fun for you maybe, but I'm enjoying it this way." Galena crawled over and sat down beside him, handing him a piece of sweet bread.

He ripped off a chunk, still glowering at the campfire. "Do you think, if you defeat Rau, and you had better beat him, I'll be able to do magic too?"

"I don't know. I've thought about it, but I don't know the answer. I guess we'll find out if we succeed. I'm trying not to think that far ahead. It feels like I'm setting myself up for failure if I do."

Elenio jerked his head once in response to this. They continued eating in silence until they finished. Deciding that it would be pointless to create a bed just for a couple of hours, they slept on the ground that night.

The next morning rays greeted Galena and Elenio as they continued their race through the forest. They ran on, determination and the knowledge that they may not make it before the crash from the energizing hit them, kept them going at a relentless pace. They continued through the day once more, sleeping a couple of hours during the night and starting before the morning dawned on the third day. It was halfway through this morning, when they heard the sound they dreaded. The clash of swords and the sound of creatures dying. Looking grimly at Elenio as they raced, Galena picked up the pace and ran faster than she ever had. Tark was out there.

Chapter Four

Tark stood in front of all the elves, eyeing the enemy across the stream with a fierce determination. Morak's archers sent word that the dark beasts were preparing to strike that morning. It was a fact Tark already knew from Mira's warnings the night before. Morak and his group were hidden strategically throughout the valley hills, posed and ready to strike from afar. Tark looked back and saw Taura eyeing the torlics and earagos with distaste and hatred. Morgo stood on his other side. He too looked grim, but ready, passing his sword from one hand to the other.

It was what they'd been training for and yet, Tark felt sorely lacking. There had not been any word or sighting of Galena. That morning, before the sun even peeked above the land of Tomiro, Tark instructed Morgo to pull up an image of Galena. As far as they could tell, she was running at an incredible speed with Elenio close to her. However, as far as their exact location, they could see nothing other than they were in the woods somewhere. Even knowing she was on her way wasn't exactly helpful.

Tark took his blade out of the scabbard and glanced down the row of elves on either side of him. He saw several scared faces, but many more wore expressions of the deepest loathing. There were plenty of signs indicating they were nervous, such as the relentless swaying back and forth as well as the continued glancing to the left and right at their neighbors. Tark expected nothing less and even had to stop himself from displaying the same nervous manners. He felt as the leader, he should display a calm demeanor, even though his insides continually threatened to explode from him.

27

Switching his blade to his dominant hand, he regarded the torlics in front of him. They sneered at him, pointing and laughing openly at them. The earagos, standing a little ways off, looked menacingly at the different elves. As far as he could see on the other side of the bank, stood monsters. There were narooks, earagos, torlics, and every other imaginable dark creature, all prepared to attack at a moment's notice. Blades glinted and flashed in the weak morning light. He watched as they shifted and moved, anxiously awaiting for some signal telling them they could charge. When he glanced around at his own smaller army, he felt his heart sink. They covered roughly the area directly surrounding their side of the bank and no more. They needed more help, but there was none to be had. If they somehow survived this ordeal, it would be by the hands of the gods.

Somewhere in the distance, he heard the first dark creature bellow a loud battle cry, causing the rest of its comrades to respond in kind, as they charged across the stream toward the elves on the other side. *Here we go*, he thought.

Tark ran toward the oncoming Torlic and met him head on, swinging his blade out and up, burying it deep within the great brute's vivid, red belly. Pulling it out, he blocked the next oncoming sword, before spinning around and taking the leg off the creature attacking him. Everywhere he turned; there was another dark creature attacking one elf or another. Eyes searching, he quickly found Taura and his heart swelled with pride. She was holding her own and others' as well. His father would have been pleased. She twisted around, cutting the hand off a narooks, and beheading another with the same swipe. She caught his eye for a moment and smiled briefly before thrusting her sword into the leg of a Torlic charging her.

Cutting down two more attacking creatures, he looked out of the corner of his eye and saw Morgo taking on a giant earagos with the help of Fala, Hasa, and Weila. Fala struck repeatedly with brute strength, while Hasa and Weila became the winds of destruction they were known to be. They slashed, swiped, and moved all before the earagos could think to swat at the place they'd been. Wherever Morgo's sword struck, caught flame immediately causing the earagos to become angrier and rasher with every moment. Arrows pelted its back from different directions above and burst into flames when they became imbedded into its flesh, causing it further pain. It had been Tark's idea to cause the arrows to catch fire as soon as they met flesh of anything, but Morgo took the thought a step further and decided it would also be beneficial for swords to be embedded with the same kind of fire. This idea took hold immediately and with the help of Pangoro, they accomplished this task in a little under a day.

Tark hacked down a narooks and two more torlics, blood spraying him from every direction. *We're pushing the enemy lines back. We're holding our own,* Tark thought with grim satisfaction.

A savage smile alighted his face and he cried out a wild battle cry before attacking a torlic that was retreating slightly. He jumped up and swung out, taking the head from his shoulders as he did so. He landed lightly on his feet, the head of his victim laying uselessly beside him, the body crashing down in front of him. He heard the sound of an earagos crashing behind him. Apparently, Morgo and the others were successful. The air around him was filled with the scent of blood and gore. Everywhere Tark turned, he saw evidence of it. From what he could tell by a quick glance, none of his elves were seriously injured in the fray.

It was then he heard screams filled with panic in his mind before he heard them fill the valley all around. Fear surged through his stomach and he felt the air in his throat constrict painfully. Looking up and around, his nightmare became a reality. A smiling earagos held his prize, Taura, by her neck. She scrabbled with the giant fingers that squeezed tighter with her struggles, causing her to still and focus on saving her own life. Tark tried to send calming thoughts to his love, but her mind was filled with fear. To his dismay, panic took hold and he found himself sprinting toward her at full pace. The earagos must have caught her from behind. She was facing Tark, her eyes full of fear.

Tark leaped into the air, intent on taking the head of this giant beast, but crashed into a wall of blackness. He fell to the ground, his body throbbing painfully from the impact. Morgo was getting up beside him and moving every bit as slowly. He apparently saw Taura's situation as well and was attempting to come to her aid too. Tark got up quickly, but found he could not move. His arms and legs were held tight by the same blackness he'd crashed into. An icy feeling crept around his neck and squeezed menacingly as he struggled to free himself. He could feel the life draining from Taura, but could do nothing to help.

Looking around as much as the icy blackness around his neck would allow, he saw every elf within sight seemed to be in the same predicament. Even the archer elves, so carefully hidden, had stopped shooting. To his relief, the enemy had also stopped fighting, but they stood staring at the sky. A great, black cloud unlike anything Tark had ever seen formed above the earagos's head.

Tark watched in horror as every shadow within the valley raced to the sky to join with the ever-growing, black mass. It stretched its smoky tentacles in every direction until the once blue sky was dark. Directly above the earagos, a giant face took shape. Its massive, black eyes the size of dinner table tops, peered down at the elves before smiling cruelly at them. It held the essence of fear itself and Tark quaked in spite of himself. Glancing toward Morgo, he saw the same fear there on his features. Dreading what was to come; he returned his gaze back to Taura and continued his struggles against the shadowy hands trapping him. He would not give up.

"Behold your future!" the face of Rau bellowed, indicating the struggling figure of Taura bellow.

If Tark's hands had been free, he would have covered his ears in pain. As it was, he had to take the full force of Rau's voice. It was deep and menacing, causing the rocks surrounding them to shake and shatter with the sheer volume of it. He groaned in pain, feeling his ears pop ominously.

"You are nothing compared to me! Did you really think you could come even close to defeating me? What chance did you have if your ancestors in their prime could not win? I will crush the life from you like this elf."

Tark's eyes rolled back; the pain of his eardrums bursting caused him to black out momentarily. He felt the hot stickiness of blood and other fluids flowing from his ears and down his neck.

"Fools, first I will deal with you and then I will deal with those you left behind, thinking them safe," the giant being spat out in disgust.

This time, Tark was relieved to find the voice sounded muffled, as if it was underwater. He heard Rau chuckle mercilessly.

"I shall begin with this one."

Tark watched with a horrified feeling as the earagos holding his love, begin to squeeze harder. Taura kicked and thrashed, her movements becoming weaker and weaker. Tark tried to yell, but the shadow at his throat prevented him. He saw Morgo twitching beside him, his face red from concentration, but to no avail. Rau prevented them from any means of escape or the ability to fight back. Tears streamed down Tark's face while he continued his fight against the shadows, he would never give up. Taura's voice begin to fade in his mind as her life started dwindling away. He fought harder. He had to get loose. The shadow around his throat tightened until he could no longer breathe himself. Catching Taura's eye, he watched her even as she focused on him. He was determined he would not take his eyes off her until he himself passed into the Land of the Gods.

* * * *

Galena raced through the forest, following the sound of the swords striking one another. Branches and brush reached out at her from all directions, scratching every exposed body part and pulling at her clothing, but she took no notice. She had to get there before something happened to Tark or any of her friends. On she ran, the sounds of battle getting louder with each step. She heard Elenio crashing through the forest somewhere behind her, but she didn't stop or even slow to check where. She had to get there. They needed her. Mira warned her that her timing was essential; they would not succeed without her. On she raced, the grunts and shouts encouraging her forward. She sped past the last tree and into the clearing before the valley. She could see a hill rising up just before the valley edge ahead of her when all went quiet. It was an eerie kind of silence. One that sent chills down her back and caused the hair on her head to prickle uncomfortably.

"Behold your future!" boomed an incredible voice.

Galena stopped dead in her tracks, clamping her hands over her ears at the first syllable.

"You are nothing compared to me! Did you really think you could come even close to defeating me? What chance do you have if your

31

ancestors in their prime could not win? I will crush the life from you like this elf."

Galena pressed her hands over her ears even harder, but even that couldn't stop the terrible voice from making her ears ache. She crouched low to the ground, trying to hide from the voice that echoed all around and even seemed to vibrate within her chest. She glanced around at Elenio and saw that he too was covering his ears. He grimaced at her when the booming voiced called out once more.

"Fools, first I will deal with you and then I will deal with those that you left behind, thinking them safe. I shall begin with this one."

Panic took hold of Galena then as she thought of all the elves below. Risking her hearing, she removed her pack and throwing it to the ground where she crouched; she got up and raced toward the hill. Coming to the edge, she halted and took in the sight below. On one side of the stream bank were hundreds of elves all in various states of being held by something unseen, although Galena had a good guess at what was keeping them from attacking. Across from the elves as well as intermingled with them were thousands of dark creatures. There were torlics, narooks, earagos, and other horrifying creatures. They made the land and all their surroundings appear black and frightening. Above it was a dark, shadowy mass. It was in this that Galena saw the face of Rau and knew where the voice came from. She clenched her fists angrily as she took in the whole of the situation. She watched for a moment as the face that covered the entirety of the battlegrounds, smiled wickedly down at an earagos. It had to be the same one Galena assumed would be crushing the life out of an elf as Rau instructed when Galena realized with a jolt, the elf swinging lifelessly from its clutches was Taura.

She pulled the Sword of Lumina from its scabbard, readying it for what was to come. Instantly, she felt the tingle of energy flow through her from the blade, making her feel even more alive than her energizing magic had. *This could be addictive,* she thought to herself. Causing a great gale of wind to pick her up, it followed the image in her mind, sweeping her over the heads of all the elves within the valley. She saw eyes from everywhere widen in response to her sudden appearance as she flew past them. Smiles begin to appear on otherwise fearful faces when they realized who it was. Flying faster than she had ever tried before, she crossed the valley in a matter of seconds, slowing only when she neared her target. Stopping the wind completely when she was within a foot of the looming giant, she landed gracefully in front of him.

"How about you start with me first," she snarled right before she plunged the Sword of Lumina into the belly of the earagos. She let go of the blade when it grew too hot to handle and stepped back, watching with great interest at what was to come. The giant monster looked down in shock at the sword sticking from his belly. Tiny cracks spread like wild fire from the sword out until they covered his entire body causing him to loosen his grip on Taura. This allowed her to slip to the ground where she collapsed into a small heap. The cracks widened, light spilling from each one. With a final groan of pain, the creature burst into thousands of pieces, light replacing the area that he had once darkened.

Reaching her hand out, the sword flew back to her. Grabbing it out of the air, she swung it back and up prepared for whatever was to come. However, the enemy stayed where they were and regarded her warily as she stood eyeing them with a fury that would not be matched. She looked up at the giant cloud, which still loomed above, but now held a look of horror where glee had been just moments before. She smiled wickedly up at it.

"Miss me?" Galena called out sarcastically. Reaching out a hand, she caused the entire valley to light up with a light so bright, both elves and monster alike had to shield their eyes or risk being blinded. A scream filled with pain and agony echoed off the valley walls and sent even the dark creatures to their knees, their own ears bleeding from the intensity of it. Galena gasped in pain as her own hearing spiked and then went painfully dull. With the final echoes of screams dying away and the disappearance of Rau, Galena caused the light to fade. She glanced briefly at the enemy and saw with some satisfaction that they were struggling to get to their feet. Taking advantage of their temporary recovery and confusion, she looked for Tark among the recovering elves. They were all smiling at her and waving their thanks for her assistance.

The elves seemed to be recovering much more quickly than the creatures of the dark. She saw Tark run over to Taura where he flipped her over once he arrived at her side. She watched him until he nodded at her, letting her know that Taura was alive. He picked her up and carried her off to safety while Galena brought Elenio down with another gust of wind so he could stand next to her in battle. Returning her gaze to the enemy, she heard the elves coming up behind her and preparing for battle once more. Morgo came and stood next to her. She nodded in appreciation before regarding the recovering torlics directly in front of her.

The enemy regained their footing, but looked shocked and a little disturbed at the outcome of their master's arrival and sudden departure. They seemed unsure of what they were to do and looked to each other for some kind of confirmation. Smiling menacingly, Galena readied her sword once more and charged. The battle cry of every elf in the valley filled her with awe beyond words. The elves had had enough and they were ready to take back their lives.

As one, the elves attacked. Morgo swung his blade out, striking down an oncoming narook that had managed to wrap its whip-like fingers around another elf. He grinned at Galena and headed off toward a group of torlics chasing down another elf. Galena decided her talents would be best applied to the oncoming earagos because of the sheer number of elves it took to beat one. Using her hand, she swept another group of dark creatures high into the air and far out of the valley before sending them crashing to the ground. Two more brave torlics charged her, one from each side. Elenio engaged one. He dropped to the ground and sweeping a leg out, knocked the legs out from under the beast. He cut the head off as the great creature went crashing to the ground, spraying him with blood.

Galena easily blocked the first blow of the second torlic with her sword. Sliding her sword down the length of the torlics blade, she spun around and behind the torlic, piercing him in the back. Instantly, the torlic burst into thousands of fragments from the contact with the sword of light; gaining the attention of three earagos, who were storming their way over to her just like she hoped. She knew Rau would want these creatures to handle the biggest threats as they could do the most damage. She figured she should have been flattered that three of them decided it was necessary to engage her.

Elenio came up behind her and prepared himself for the onslaught, but Galena stopped him saying, "I need you to make sure no one else tries to join in our fun. Can you watch my back from the other monsters while I'm focused on these three? I'm sure the other creatures are not above attacking me while I'm busy and I'm going to need to focus entirely on these." She eyed the oncoming earagos while she waited for Elenio's response.

"I can help..." he started, but she stopped him by placing a hand over his mouth.

"Please do that for me. I will be fine and you know it."

"The archers are already taking care of the torlics or anything else."

"They can't see everything coming for me. I need to know I don't have to worry about any sneak attacks while I'm otherwise engaged."

Elenio made to say more, but the roar of one of the giant beasts stopped him.

Galena turned to look at them, her face alight with the inner glow the Sword of Lumina provided. Her expression was dangerous. It would have stopped most creatures dead in their tracks, but not the earagos. However, that could've been the fact they had poor vision.

Doing as Galena had asked, Elenio stepped back, placing a hand on Morgo's shoulder as the elf attempted to join in on the fray. He indicated with his sword the oncoming narooks and torlics and the two of them took off in the direction of those monsters.

Galena gave a practice swing, making the earagos back up rather than touch the dreaded blade. They circled around her, swinging their clubs at her in an alternating pattern. Galena batted these away with ease. They were scared and she knew it. Standing straight, she sent a bolt of lightning down from the sky, striking one of the earagos directly on the head. He fell to the ground, dead.

The other two charged her, thinking she would be preoccupied, but found out otherwise. She spun around, cutting the foot off one and causing it to erupt into a brilliant display of light and body parts. The third stopped dead in its tracks, fear apparent in its frozen expression. Galena swung her blade in a circular fashion before she chased after the earagos, who had suddenly realized engaging her in battle was a very foolish idea indeed.

"I don't think so," she muttered under her breath. Flinging her hand up, she caused several boulders to rise up and pursue the giant. They crashed into its legs, pitching the giant forward and onto his face. He rolled over quickly, his legs not quite following him as they should have and held up his club threateningly. Galena was unmoved by the gesture. Taking the tip of her sword, she pierced the creature's toe. The effect was immediate. Within moments, the earagos shared the same fate as so many other dark creatures that met the Sword of Lumina. Darkness never survives the light.

Chapter Five

Elenio ran up beside Galena, hacking down a retreating creature, with no name for it on his way over. He was grinning broadly at her, pride emanating from his every gesture. Galena watched several other creatures flying through the air, evidence the underground elves were at work. Together, Elenio and Galena battled on; their backs always to one another as they slew the rippling, black mass that was Rau's army. No more dark creatures pursued her, but as a whole, seemed to retreat with every step she took toward them.

In every direction Galena looked, she saw elves fighting against the dark. Streams of blood flowed over the rocky soil and the ground became littered with the dead and injured bodies of their enemy. She saw several elves littered throughout the dark creatures as well, most with severe injuries, some not moving at all. These elves concerned Galena greatly, and with a gust of wind she picked several groups of them up and sent them flying toward the safety of the camp. She did this several more times until she was sure she had gotten most of them.

Returning to the fray, she continued her onslaught against Rau's army, determined to make a dent in the giant, black mass. When she cut down one creature, she found another one had appeared in its place.

She saw elves fighting in pairs and the underground elves using magic. The rate at which they used magic was becoming less and less as the battle raged on though. At one point, Galena found herself flying an elf to safety when he dropped to the ground, out cold from the use of too much power.

Hearing a grunt of pain, Galena turned to find Elenio on his knees doing his best to ward off an attacking torlic and failing miserably. He had a deep gash on his upper arm and a nasty cut on his cheek. He looked completely drained. Galena swung her blade out and cutting the torlic in half from the shoulder to hip, she watched as the monster began falling to the ground, but disintegrated into ash instead as light burst from him. Elenio looked up at her wearily, his face and clothing covered in blood.

"Your magic has worn off," he managed to say in-between pants.

Galena looked alarmed and realized she had been using the sword's strength instead of her own. Now that Elenio pointed it out, she realized she was a great deal more tired than she had been at the start. Tark came up to them at that moment, looking around them as he did.

"Galena we need a break. Nigora is at her wits end with all the elves you sent her way and there are many more elves injured. We need time to regroup," he said, bending over to pick up another injured elf just feet away.

Galena nodded wearily, not sure how to, but knowing he meant she needed to scare the enemy enough to get them to retreat. *Fine*, she thought. *Time to end this battle.*

Elenio grabbed her hand before she strode off, intent on ending this battle for the time being. "You can still overdo it, Galena, remember that."

Her eyes softened and she gave his hand a gentle squeeze. She took a moment to heal his injuries quickly before she sent him flying toward the safety of the camp along with Tark and the injured elf with a wave of her hand. She took a deep breath before heading off to where the enemy numbers were the thickest.

Running at as much of a sprint as she could manage at that moment, she hurdled over bodies and twirled around others, cutting down anything that crossed her path. Often times, she found herself intervening in what would have been unfortunate outcomes for the elves fighting several dark creatures at once. She received many cuts and stabs, some more serious than others, but nothing stopped her. Finally reaching a point where every type of dark creature Rau sent out surrounded her, she stopped. This was exactly where she wanted to be. Seeing this glowing elf in the midst of their allies, the dark creatures advanced on her, unsure how she had gotten there, but not caring just the same. Galena smiled. Her plan so far was working.

"If you're a friend of the elves, flee now," Galena shouted as loudly as she could. She watched the enemy advance toward her slowly and the few elves that had been within earshot run for their camp. *Mira be with me,* she thought dully. Quickly sheathing her blade, Galena stood, bringing up with her hands a great spiraling wind that sucked up several of the surrounding creatures. She sent many of them colliding into one another breaking bones and smashing bodies in the process. Several more within her view, caught fire and could be heard screaming over the wailing winds and shouts of the flying creatures. Huge bolts of lightning came sizzling from the sky and into the massive crowd of darkness causing explosions throughout, sending bodies in many directions and lighting up the darkening sky. Picking up boulders from the valley walls with the wind, she sent them flying around and into the bodies of many more creatures. The screams of pain and agony could be heard as they vibrated through the air and the ground trembled with the retreating army. She heard a horn somewhere in the background, indicating Rau's army was indeed pulling back. Sending more bolts of lightning chasing after them in case any of them had second thoughts, she crashed to the ground on her knees. With the Sword of Lumina put away, the bone-crushing weariness crashed over her and she blacked out.

Galena registered two things when she opened her eyes. The first was the fact she felt like a tribe of earagos had trampled over her. Every inch of her body ached and she was sure her head was on the verge of exploding. The second was that although she heard voices in the background, they sounded strangely muffled. With sudden clarity, she recalled the events leading up to the present with the exception of how she had gotten to where she was. Thinking of the small pieces of the ear that allowed a person to hear, she healed the holes in them. As the warm tingly feel passed, she could hear the voices more clearly.

"If she doesn't wake soon, I'm getting Nigora again," Elenio said quietly.

"Nigora said she's fine as far as she could tell, just worn out. It won't do any good to bring her back so she can tell us exactly the same thing," Tark whispered back.

"But what…" Elenio started.

Galena cut him short by sitting up. "Peace Elenio. I'm fine, although I wouldn't be surprised if I found one of you took advantage of the fact I was out cold and rolled a large boulder over me."

With the act of sitting up, Galena's head gave a particularly nasty throb. Fighting the urge to be sick, Galena concentrated on the muscles that were causing the headache and eased the tension there. Instantly, Galena felt relief as the headache first eased and then faded altogether. "Okay," she said sighing deeply as she regarded Elenio, Tark, and Taura who were all sitting in what appeared to be a tent, with her. "Now, can somebody explain to me how I got here and what has happened since I've been out?" Waves of anger that were not her feelings, washed over her. Clearly, Elenio was not happy. She assumed it had something to do with the fact she caused herself to blackout once more. Raising a hand to stop Elenio before he even started, "I know what your thoughts are, but wait to tell me off. Right now, I want to know if the enemy did actually retreat and where I am."

Elenio looked furious. Standing up, he stormed out of the tent. Galena watched him go, feeling upset, but knowing he would cool off in time. She turned to look at Tark and Taura once more and found them both smiling at her.

"For your first question, Morgo brought you here after you passed out. This is Elenio and your tent. Next, yes, the enemy retreated thanks to your brilliant display of power. They are currently camping within a mile of here. We imagine they plan on heading back to Blackwell soon, versus going against you again, but only time will tell. You slept through the night and most of the morning, but you seem to be recovering well. Be easy on Elenio, he's had a rough night," Tark finished, looking down at the ground as he said this.

"I know, but I needed answers first. We don't have the time or the luxury of throwing fits every time I push myself a little too hard."

"How would you have felt if the roles had been reversed?"

Galena flinched as the memory of Elenio pushing a sword through himself flashed through her mind.

"Exactly."

"You're right. I'll apologize to him." Galena stood, healing the tender muscles as she did so and walked over to Tark. She bent down and wrapped her arms around him, hugging him tightly before whispering, "I missed you something fierce, big brother." He returned the hug, standing as he did so. Letting go of him, she turned to Taura. She went to hug her as well when she saw the dark bruising around her neck and noted the way she seemed to struggle to swallow properly. Galena thought of the broken blood vessels healing themselves and the swollen muscles and tendons returning to normal. She repaired the holes in her eardrums as well.

Taura's eyes widened as the pain eased and disappeared. Taking a practice swallow, she smiled brightly at Galena before jumping up and wrapping her arms around her sister-in-law.

"Anything else hurting?" Galena whispered.

Taura shook her head and hugged her even tighter. "It's been a long time, my sister." She laid her head on Galena's shoulder and she smiled.

"How about you big brother, any major problems?"

"Everyone has busted eardrums, and some elves sustained some pretty serious injuries, but Nigora is dealing with those along with some of the underground elves that didn't pass out from too much magic use. Taura, as you know, was in rough shape, but she refused to be helped for fear of someone else coming in with bigger wounds. Nigora can only do so much before she wears out too, unlike some elves we know." He reached over and messed Galena's hair to which she retreated.

"Just because I missed you, doesn't mean I won't stick you in a tree for annoying me. Just ask Elenio. Plus, I obviously can wear myself out too." She smiled at him and taking a moment, healed his ears as well.

He opened his mouth wide and rotated his jaw when she had finished, causing his newly repaired eardrum to pop. "Thanks and now if you'll excuse me, I've already received several messages requiring my attention that I've been putting off until I was sure you were okay." Wrapping his arms around her once more, he hugged her briefly before he walked out of the tent. Taura smiled at Galena and then followed Tark out, leaving Galena alone with her thoughts.

She concentrated on the camp of elves as a whole. Making a great effort for she had never attempted something so big at once, she thought of every ear healing and sound returning to normal. Instantly, she felt a huge drop in her energy level and she swayed ominously where she stood. *That can't be good*, she thought as the weariness of overuse made her feel light headed and sick. Putting her head in her hands again, she fought to remain conscious, knowing Elenio would be back any moment and the last thing she needed was to give him another reason to be mad. Walking slowly back to her hammock, she sat, feeling extremely disoriented when she did. *Oh great*, she thought when everything went black once more.

* * * *

Galena opened her eyes to find herself surrounded by darkness. She blinked a couple of times, but found the darkness remained. Rubbing her eyes wearily, she sat up and waited for her eyes to adjust to the night. Looking around, she found herself still in the tent Tark assigned to Elenio and her. She tried to stand, but stopped when she heard a rustling somewhere across the room. She squinted hoping to make out something in the dark, but all she saw was a large shape. Walking slowly over to the dark mass, she found Elenio, his head in his hands, asleep in the chair. Shaking him gently, he stirred and then sat up quickly, looking quite alarmed at having fallen asleep in the first place.

"What is it?" he asked, searching the darkness for anything out of the ordinary.

"Come to bed, or the hammock, or whatever you want to call it," Galena whispered to him.

"You did it again, didn't you?"

"I don't know what you're talking about," Galena said a little too innocently.

"Everyone's ears healing." He looked at her dully, clearly trying to contain the anger Galena felt radiating from him.

Galena sighed, knowing she'd been caught. Crouching down, she looked up at him and placed a hand on the side of his face. She tried to smooth the tightness around his eyes away with her thumb, but to no avail. He placed his own hand on hers, stilling her movements.

"I'm sorry."

"That doesn't help."

"I know, but I don't know what else to say."

"Try something like, you'll never do something that stupid again," he said bitterly.

"Then I would be lying."

He removed his hand from hers angrily and looked away, but not before Galena saw the bitterness there.

"Elenio, you know I had to do something or we would have lost. Everyone was wearing out."

He continued to stare at the far wall, refusing to acknowledge her.

"Elenio, nothing happened. I no longer have the marks that would kill me if I use too much magic."

"Then why did you black out again?" Elenio shouted, finally deciding to look at her as he did.

"Remember what Morgo told us in the underground world? Using magic is like exercising, you can only do so much before your body shuts itself down to recuperate. My blacking out was my body's way of telling me it needed a break. Other than tired, I'm fine."

Understanding dawned on Elenio's face as he smiled weakly at her. "I forgot about that bit of information. Old habits die hard, I guess."

Galena returned the smile, glad that was over. "Between all the fighting, my energizing wearing off, and the amount of magic I used without holding my sword, I was more than tired. Lucky for you, I'm extremely stubborn." She raised up slightly and kissed him gently.

"And incredibly powerful."

"Has anything new happened?" she asked, purposefully ignoring the last statement. She stood up and walked back over to the hammock, her muscles stiff from crouching.

"Well, while you were sleeping the day away, Rau's army started packing up. We believe they are heading out in the morning and Tark does not intend to let them get far. He wants to give you a day to fully recover from all the exercise you have attempted the last several days. As well as the underground elves, who don't possess quite as much magic as you, but are helpful none the less." Elenio got up and walked over to the other side of the hammock where he gingerly sat down.

"I'll be ready to go first thing tomorrow."

"Yes, but the other magical elves will not. Don't worry. We know which way they're headed." Elenio laid back and pulled Galena down with him. "If it makes you feel better, we can follow at a distance and pick them off along with Morak's group."

"It would make me feel useful," Galena said, while staring thoughtfully at the ceiling.

"If you want to feel useful, I'm sure Nigora could use your help. Many elves were seriously injured. Nigora has already taken care of most of them, but there are several more in need of assistance. Nothing life threatening mind you, but there was still enough work to be done that Nigora couldn't accomplish it all in one day. She wore herself out and has been sleeping ever since yesterday afternoon."

Galena thought about this for a moment, deciding that getting as many elves in the best condition as possible made more sense. Plus, it would give her a chance to stay with Tark and Taura for a bit longer before battling more of the dark creatures.

"We should stay and do what we can for the elves here," she said yawning.

"I was hoping you would say that," Elenio said, a hint of a smile in his voice.

"Yeah, I kind of thought you would." Galena elbowed his side playfully, which almost sent both of them flying off the hammock with the movement.

"Haven't you done enough damage today?" Elenio asked when they had gotten the hammock under control.

Galena smiled sheepishly into his shoulder, but said nothing. Closing her eyes, she felt herself drifting off into a dreamless sleep.

Galena awoke to find herself alone in the hammock. Weak morning rays shone through the thin material walls of the tent. Forgetting how flimsy a hammock was, she sat up quickly, which resulted in her being flipped onto the floor in an undignified position. It was in this position that Tark walked in and saw her. Upon seeing her lying face up on the floor, legs tangled in the makeshift bed, Tark burst into laughter, unable to regain control for several minutes.

Realizing Tark would be absolutely no help, Galena began the process of untangling her legs, but with little success. Finally, taking pity on her, Tark assisted her, laughing all the while.

"Have you seen Elenio?" Galena asked, hoping to get Tark to think of anything else to stop him from laughing, but her efforts were in vain.

Tark simply shook his head, but continued laughing, wiping the tears from his eyes as he did so. Rolling her eyes, Galena stormed out of the tent, grumbling all the while.

She stepped out into the bright light and blinked a few times to keep her eyes from watering as she searched the surrounding elves for any sign of Elenio. She saw several elves she recognized, all who wanted to take a few minutes and chat with her, but she didn't stop for long. She could sense Elenio somewhere nearby, but couldn't be sure exactly where. Feeling frustrated, she turned around, intent on heading back to their tent. *He can come and find me,* she thought. Not paying a bit of attention to where she was headed, she collided with another elf, sending them both sprawling backward. *This is not my day for looking graceful or like I know what I'm doing,* Galena thought, feeling even more annoyed at herself than anything.

Sitting up, she groaned slightly, intending to apologize to her unknown victim when she realized who it was. "MORAK!" Quickly getting to her feet, she reached out a hand, which he gratefully took, and pulled him to his feet.

"I was hoping to run into you, just not literally," he said grinning broadly.

Galena blushed profusely and looked at the ground.

"Are you heading out to fend off another horde of evil creatures?" he asked.

"No, I'm in search of Elenio. You haven't seen him have you?" she asked, still looking at the ground.

"Yeah, he stopped in to see Nigora while I was with her. She told him where he could find Morgo."

"Are you alright?" Galena asked, looking him over for any signs of ailments that she could help with, especially after their collision.

"Took a nasty fall out of a tree Tark put me in after you sent Rau running. Guess I wasn't prepared to be freed so quickly and when I was,

I wasn't ready. Fell and broke my ankle. Nigora did her best, but I get the impression I have some healing to do on my own." Morak looked at his ankle with the same annoyance Galena felt just moments before with herself.

Focusing her attention on the ankle, she thought of the bone regrowing, the tendons tightening back to normal and the swelling all around the bone and muscle reducing. She healed the broken blood vessels and the muscles connecting to the bone. Satisfied his ankle was as good as new, she looked up and found the same look of awe she had seen so many times on Tark and Elenio or any other elf she had helped.

"Better?" she asked.

"It's true then, isn't it? You're more powerful than any other elf that has walked the land of Tomiro."

"It appears so," she said sighing heavily. "Well, I need to find Elenio."

"Okay, Morgo's tent is that way," he said, pointing in the direction she originally felt Elenio's presence. "Thanks again."

"No problem." Galena gave him a hug before heading back in the direction of the tent Morak pointed out. She missed how everyone used to treat her before they discovered she could use magic. Then, everyone had known her as Melan and Tark's little sister and treated her as such. Now, it was almost as if the only thing they could think of when they were around her was her magical ability. *Someday, hopefully everything will go back to the way it was,* she thought. *Either that or I won't be around anymore for elves to treat differently. One way or the other, things would change, come what may.*

Chapter Six

"Anyone home?" Galena called at the tent Morak indicated belonged to Morgo. Elenio opened the flap and smiled at her. She couldn't help it; she returned the smile and reaching up, kissed him quickly on the lips.

"I missed seeing your irritated face when I woke up," she whispered.

"Am I forgiven for acting like a pain yesterday?" he whispered back, smiling as he did so.

"Always." She kissed him quickly once more before stepping past him and into the tent. She found Morgo, shirtless and smiling up at her from his own hammock. The last time Galena saw him was during the battle. She really hadn't been paying attention to him and the way he'd changed since leaving him behind in the world he knew. When they last parted, it was at the entrance to the outside world near the base of the Mountains of the Gods. She couldn't remember exactly how he had looked because he had been so utterly forgettable that often times she found her thoughts drifting in all directions at once. The longer she was with him, the more these forgettable traits faded. Even then, she realized other than the dull and ghostlike look that was common among the underground elves; she could remember nothing else of his appearances.

Now, as she looked at him, she realized he'd lost the pale, white skin and the limp, dull dark hair. She was surprised to discover how handsome he really was. His skin had darkened up, even in the winter months, to a more creamy color and his hair, which hung below his shoulders, was now a dark brown instead of the black it once appeared to be. His eyes held the biggest change, as they were full of life. They even had a mischievous quality to them. His smile was warm and friendly and Galena found herself returning his smile easily.

"I'd get up to greet you properly, but as you can see, I'm a little ill-disposed at the moment," he said, indicating the bleeding bandage at his side she somehow missed before.

"Couldn't Nigora help you more than that?" Galena asked, a little shocked he wasn't in better condition.

"She could, but I wouldn't let her. There were other elves in worse condition than I was and she needed all the energy she could muster at the time. I bandaged myself up and told her I would wait until she took care of the elves whose needs were more critical than mine." He grimaced horribly as he attempted to readjust himself so he could look at her more comfortably.

"Weren't you the one who brought me to my tent?" Galena asked feeling clearly confused.

"That didn't take physical strength. I just flew you back with the wind. Nina helped some too," he said, grimacing slightly as he readjusted yet again.

"Hold still and I'll get you fixed up. We can't have my former mentor all banged up."

He rolled his eyes at this statement, further evidence of the changes the above world had on him. Sitting down across from Morgo, Elenio chuckled at their friend's reaction, but said nothing more. Galena shook her head, amazed with the changes in Morgo. Placing her hand on the wound, she healed the damage to his inner organs, the muscles, and the surrounding tissue. She replaced his loss of blood, taking care not to energize him with the addition of too much oxygen and nutrients to the newly replaced fluid. Finally, she repaired the skin, making it appear as if he'd never been wounded.

Morgo looked down and seeing his stomach whole once more, looked up at Galena with a huge grin on his face before commenting, "You've come a long ways since the last time we met." He put on a shirt, stood up, and stretched from side to side, twisting his waist this way and that to test the job Galena did. "Amazing, I feel better than I have in a long while."

Still smiling, he sat back down while gesturing for Galena to sit in an empty chair next to Elenio. Morgo waited for Galena to sit before asking, "So how do you like life in the center of everyone's attention?"

He winked at her conspiratorially, which stopped Galena from saying anything rude.

"You certainly are quite a bit different from the last time we met." Galena laughed.

"The upper world agrees with me. Elenio was just describing how everyone has been asking for you since your grand appearance at our most recent battle and we already know Rau is searching for you as evidenced by the massive army he sent. What have you learned about yourself since the last time that we talked? What theory have you discovered to be the correct one?"

Galena thought back to the conversation they had in the underground world in one of the many tunnels they traveled while they were there. It seemed a lifetime ago. In reality, she knew it couldn't have been more than a couple of months, maybe a little longer. Morgo threw out two different theories as far as why Galena had been able to do magic even with the marks of Rau on her hands and feet. The first theory he had was the idea there were flaws in her tattoos. They'd almost immediately rejected this idea, but were not entirely sure. His second theory was she contained more magic in her than most normal elves. This idea seemed more fitting, but once again, they were unsure.

When Elenio and Tark took her to the healing waters at Mira's View, it had been there Mira removed the marks of Rau from her hands and feet, explaining to Galena she was indeed more powerful than any elf had ever been. She explained to Galena, she contained more magic than a hundred elves combined. Galena had not believed this at first, but after the last couple of months, she realized what Mira told her was true.

"The second proved to be correct. I have it on good authority from Mira herself," Galena said, training her eyes on the floor. Once again, the conversation came back to her power.

"Don't worry, your fame will pass. When we underground elves first showed up, we were the talk of the village as well, but once everyone adjusted to our magical abilities, our fame passed and we became just another elf. Your popularity may take a little longer to die out, especially after the show you put on, but take heart, it will pass, of this I am confident," Morgo said quietly to her.

She returned her gaze back to his face and saw the sincerity there. She nodded in thanks, but said nothing to this. She hoped he was right, just as he had been with his theories concerning her.

Elenio reached over and taking her hand gave it a little squeeze, further reassuring her.

"Now, while we're on the topic of your magical abilities. Remember another conversation we had before about elves having talents in one area or another with their magical abilities. I think I told you my strength was in the area of putting people to sleep just as Nigora's magical ability is definitely in the area of healing. It would seem you have no limit to a specific skill either. Am I wrong?" Morgo looked at her, a hint of a smile on his face as he waited for an answer.

"I'd forgotten about that particular conversation," Galena said, thoughtfully looking up at the ceiling of the tent. She remembered it now along with the conversation on how using magic was a lot like exercising. When you did too much, your body would shut down in order to preserve itself, which was not always ideal especially when you were in a sticky situation, such as she had been the day before. "You also mentioned you did not have the capabilities of producing fire or causing things like torlics to catch on fire, yet while we were fighting I distinctly recall you setting several creatures ablaze when you struck them with your sword," Galena retorted, a smirk now on her face.

"Aahh, no, what you saw was the work of Pangoro. Tark had the idea to put fire into arrows and I just took it a step further by having Pangoro put the fire into the swords."

Galena felt thoroughly confused at this point and looked to Elenio to see if he understood it at all either. Judging by the look on his face and the lack of thoughts on the matter, this was news to him as well.

Taking in the looks of both Elenio and Galena, Morgo laid back on his hammock and placing his hands behind his head, explained, "It's much like the floating light concept only instead of trapping light within glass orbs or frozen air, we trapped fire within the blade of the sword. Whenever the blade encounters anything, it releases some of the fire within. If you recall, as the battle raged on, I lost the capability of igniting creatures with my sword because I had used up all the fire within. The same concept went into the arrows as well. It was a difficult bit of magic to perform, and without the help of Pangoro who has been doing this for a lot longer, we may not have been able to accomplish it."

Galena's eyebrows raised with surprise. It was a good idea and made her wonder if she could accomplish the same thing with all the swords the elves used. Surely, she had enough power to do so and it would give them more of an advantage over the enemy for their next battle.

"Okay, back to my question. Is there anything you have not been able to do?" Morgo asked once more, looking to both Elenio and Galena for an answer.

Galena looked at Elenio for which he simply shook his head. She could feel his pride as well as read it in the expression on his face. "So far no. Everything I've tried has been relatively easy. I only blacked out after running for nearly three days straight and then using a ton of magic along with fighting. Moreover, I've figured out how to do a sort of energizing of our bodies. It gives us a lot of energy, but when we crash from it, we really crash. The effects from pushing our bodies so hard during the energy rush seems to be rough physically on our bodies as well. When I blacked out, my own energy rush had burnt out and I wasn't holding the Sword of Lumina, which seems to have its own energy when I'm touching it."

"Interesting," Morgo said thoughtfully.

"May I see your sword?" Galena asked, curious to see if she would be able to accomplish the same thing that Pangoro had.

"Certainly." Morgo sat up and reaching down pulled his sword from its scabbard and handed it to Galena.

Galena had been able to charge Morgo's sword with no difficulty, much to his amusement. In Galena's opinion, it was a lot easier than creating a floating light orb. A single touch with the idea of trapping fire within its breakable bounds and the task was done. Galena smiled, thinking of Morgo and Elenio's enthusiasm at the idea of her being able to do the same thing with all the other weapons the elves used. Galena felt this was an interesting concept and it would definitely edge their chances against Rau's army. *First things first*, she thought.

After bidding farewell to Morgo and Elenio, she headed in the direction Morgo had indicated Nigora's tent was. She felt getting everyone healthy as quickly as possible was a little more important at the time. Some of the elves were seriously injured and if they didn't survive their first battle, flaming swords would be of little use. Moreover, she wasn't entirely sure if she should give everyone's sword a flaming quality to it. Morgo confessed it took him several days to get (use) used to his sword as well as several serious burns. *That kind of advantage may not be for everyone,* Galena thought shaking her head bemusedly when she recalled Morgo blushing fiercely when he told her the last bit.

Galena was able to locate Nigora's tent easily considering it was the largest one and there was a line of injured elves waiting around the entrance of it. Not even bothering to call out, Galena entered the tent, passing the injured elves as she did so. There were elves lying everywhere in hammocks that had been set up for the sole purpose of dealing with the sick and injured. Galena realized why Nigora was wearing out quickly as some of the elves in the sick bed looked like they were on the verge of crossing over into the Land of the Gods.

"And Morgo said she had taken care of the extremely bad off," Galena muttered to herself as she eyed some of the worst cases. Spying Nigora checking on a more serious patient across from the entrance of the tent, Galena made her way toward her, taking a few moments here and there to heal some of the patients along the way. When she arrived at the hammock Nigora was leaning over, she grew alarmed. Nigora looked pale, even more so for an underground elf. Her skin around her face appeared to be almost gray from all the work that she had done. Sweat beaded her brow and she looked like she was on the verge of passing out herself. Galena reached for her shoulders, just as the older elf started to tilt forward, her own exhaustion getting the better of her.

"Nigora, you know better than that!" Galena scolded her as she helped the healer to a seat next to the hammock. "I'm here to help and you need to go find someplace to sleep if you're going to be any use later on."

"So many," she said wearily. "There are so many and just when I think I have gotten ahead, more come." She placed her head in her hands, clearly worn beyond what she could handle.

"Where are your sleeping quarters?" Galena asked softly.

With a shaky hand, Nigora indicated a lone hammock in the corner of the tent. Galena helped the little elf to her feet and to the hammock, she pointed out. Once she got Nigora comfortably situated, she went to work. She started with the more serious elves and worked her way through the tent. By the end of the evening, she'd started on some of the elves waiting outside for Nigora's aid. By the time Elenio arrived with a tray of food, she was beginning to feel extremely tired and famished. Galena smiled gratefully and went to him.

"You are just the elf I wanted to see," she said, kissing him quickly on the cheek.

"Yeah, that's because I come bringing gifts," he joked for he knew food was the center of her thoughts.

"True, then there is sleep, and of course my thoughts turn to you," she said grinning as she grabbed a loaf of bread and wedge of cheese from the tray.

"Always last," Elenio said in mock disgust.

"That, my love, you'll never be," Galena said, grinning broadly and causing Elenio to laugh at her when she did. She'd shoved several bites of bread and cheese into her mouth, giving her the look of a squirrel with its cheeks full of nuts. Swallowing with as much dignity as she could muster and not succeeding even in the slightest, caused Elenio to double over with laughter, tears in his eyes. Galena realized this was the second time today she caused someone so much mirth, they couldn't stop laughing at her. Galena ignored this for the most part and continued eating.

Finishing the tray in record time, she secretly hoped part of it had been Elenio's. *Would serve him right for laughing at me,* she thought irritably. It seemed every time she thought he had calmed down, he would turn to look at her and start all over. "Have we heard anything about Rau's army?" Galena asked, as she rolled her eyes at another fit of laughter on Elenio's part. That sobered him up.

"They pulled out early this morning and are making their way toward Blackwell. Tark wants to stay here another day and then pursue them." Elenio brushed some of the crumbs off the tray as he said this.

"Why are we waiting another day?"

"Some of the underground elves really overdid it. Plus, he wants to make sure you've had plenty of time to rest."

"Doesn't he realize I don't burn out like other elves?"

"Yes, but you still pushed yourself too hard and with all the healing you did today. You're going to need some quiet time of your own to be at your best."

"I'm fi..." Galena started, but stopped when Elenio raised a hand.

"I don't want to hear it. You passed out twice in a little under two days. We all know you're not going to take it easy on any dark creature you come across so yes, you're going to rest before we head out. You've taken care of everyone here today, the whole camp will attest to that, now it's time to take care of you."

Galena glared stonily at him, intent on continuing the argument.

"Galena, I know what you're thinking and you should know I'm not letting up on this. Tark agrees with me. He's the one leading this camp, so pipe down and let's get back to our own tent. The sooner you rest up, the sooner we can get going."

"You know, I'm getting tired of everyone telling me what I can and can't do." Galena sat back in the chair and crossed her arms angrily.

"Yes, because we have been able to do that so well and better yet, you always listen to us," Elenio said, rolling his eyes as he stood. He held out a hand to help Galena up, which she considered briefly ignoring. "Galena, I'm not above going to get Morgo and having him put you to sleep and dragging you back to our tent that way. We've been going full steam for the last four days you need a break. Now, let's go."

Growling in frustration, Galena knew when she was beaten, and she knew he was right. The tiredness she felt from working on so many injured elves was starting to catch up with her.

"I knew you would see things my way," Elenio said smiling when he saw her thoughts.

"Well, I guess you're bound to be right once in a while," Galena said, heaving herself to her feet and grinning mischievously at him.

"That's my girl." Taking her hand, Elenio led them back to their tent for which Galena was grateful for because she really wasn't sure which one was theirs after storming away from it early that morning.

"How's Morgo?"

"Much better as I'm sure you knew he would be after working on him. Morak is also well. Tark sent him and some of his archers out after the army to keep track of them until we catch up. Not that we'll need them to locate those brutes. It would be a little difficult to lose an army that size." Elenio shook his head, amused at his own sarcasm. "I understand you saw Tark this morning." He couldn't keep the laughter out of his voice with this last statement.

"Yeah, this wasn't my most graceful day," Galena said, hoping to ward off the fits of laughter that she was sure would come. "How far is our tent? I don't remember walking this far."

"Just over there," he said grinning, pointing in the direction of a tent on the outer edges of the camp. He knew what she was trying to do. She slapped his shoulder for good measure before walking in that direction.

"Home sweet home," Galena said, opening the flap of the tent and stepping into the dark little room. *How dreary*, she thought, letting the flap close behind her. Thinking of the floating orbs of light from Gora and the underground world, she focused on air shaped like a small ball and trapped some of the light she saw in the lightning within the confines of it. The result caused the inside of the tent to be bathed in the soft light. *That's a little better,* she thought dully.

"No sense prettying the place up if we're heading out the day after tomorrow," Elenio said as he stepped through the doorway of the tent. "Especially considering I can't see you wanting to stay in here more than to sleep."

"I really don't even want to sleep in here, to be honest. It reminds me too much of the underground world."

"It's not that bad," Elenio said, as he sat down on the hammock and stretched out.

"Do you think I should put a protective barrier around the camp?" Galena asked. She couldn't help feeling vulnerable without it, now that they were so close to Rau's army.

"No. Tark has patrols making rounds around the camp. Your job is to rest. You're the most important person in the upcoming battles. Get some sleep while you can and let others take care of you for a little while."

55

Galena shrugged and then moving slowly so as not to repeat the fiasco of earlier that morning, she sat next to Elenio. Lying back, she rolled over so that she could lay her head on his shoulder and wrap an arm around his middle. Instead of risking the movement, she caused a gentle breeze to pick up their blanket and pull it up to their shoulders. The nights had warmed up; however, it was still chilly enough that the blanket helped Galena feel nice and warm. The activities of the day ran through Galena's mind, making her feel incredibly tired and before she knew it, she was fast asleep.

* * * *

Tark awoke to the sun attempting to shine through the thick tent material. He looked over at Taura, still sleeping curled up next to him. He pulled the blanket up over her shoulders and kissed her lightly on the forehead before he quietly slipped from the hammock. He wanted to check with the night patrol and Morgo before the camp really began to wake up and stir. Slipping past the tent flap and stepping into the bright light of the morning, Tark had to blink several times, allowing his eyes to adjust to the light before he was able to continue. He talked with each of the patrols to find that the night was quiet when they started their shifts and the guards before reported the same. *Galena must have really scared Rau's army,* Tark thought grimly. Thanking the elves for their reports and work, he headed off in the direction of Morgo's tent.

When he got to it, he was surprised to see the tent flap propped wide open because the air was still chilly. Assuming since the door was open, anyone was welcome, Tark stepped into the tent. Sitting on the hammock with his back to the opening was Morgo. His head was bent and he appeared to be looking at something in his lap. Tark cleared his throat, hoping to get his attention, but Morgo remained in the same position. Tark began to worry something was wrong so he crossed over to where the elf sat and peered over his shoulder to see him holding a bowl full of water. In the water was the image of Venia. It appeared she was sitting down and staring vacantly at nothing at all, as she had so often done when Tark was around her.

"She's still beautiful, isn't she?" Tark asked. The result of him speaking when Morgo was so entranced caused both of them to be covered in water and Morgo to end up on the ground, looking up at Tark and breathing heavily. "Sorry, I tried to get your attention before, but you were a little preoccupied."

"You're right. I had no idea that you were behind me as evidenced by my reaction," Morgo said, chuckling slightly while he got up. He stood and shook his hands to get some of the excess water from them. He looked sheepishly at Tark, much like a child who had been caught doing something naughty. "I suppose you would like an explanation."

"I have an idea, but I'm willing to listen regardless," Tark said, grinning at the look on his friend's face. For in truth, Tark realized Morgo had developed some type of feelings for Venia, otherwise he wouldn't have paid as much attention to her as he had.

"She is beautiful. I've never seen anything as beautiful as Venia. The moment I laid eyes on her, I felt a pull like I had never experienced with anyone in the world from which I come from. I think the fact she is from the world above is what holds part of the attraction, but only a small part."

"Are you sure she isn't just a puzzle for you to figure out?" Tark asked smirking slightly. His friend Morgo was always trying to figure out how things worked or the reason behind anything he found intriguing. To Morgo, the world was one big mystery, waiting for him to unravel. It was the reason he'd begun collecting so many books.

"I'm not sure to be honest. That was the reason I became so interested in the first place, but then she started responding to things I was doing for her. Just little things like smiling at me or looking toward me when she heard my voice. It's gotten to the point where I look forward to those moments and find myself doing whatever it takes to cause her to smile or acknowledge me at all." Morgo sat heavily down on his hammock, looking at his hands as if they had somehow betrayed him. "I'm crazy, aren't I?" He sounded thoroughly depressed and Tark couldn't help feeling a little sorry for him.

"No, not crazy. Well, maybe not completely crazy." Tark grinned at him.

Morgo returned the smile. "You know I asked Nigora to stay behind with her, so that she could continue to try and bring her back. She refused to though. She said her talents would be needed after battles. I knew she was right, but I still couldn't help feeling disappointed when she didn't remain behind. Although, we're both at a loss for exactly what to do."

"I think you were heading in the right direction. Love her back to life."

"Are you angry at me, because we were friends first?" Morgo looked down at this, still looking sheepish.

"No, I'm not sure I completely understand, but who am I to judge others?"

Morgo gave a half grin at this, relief evident on his face. "Neither do I." Morgo shook his head a little sadly before looking up and regarding Tark. "Now, how can I help you, since I assume your main purpose for coming to visit was not to scare the wits out of me?"

"No, but it was definitely a perk," Tark said, laughing at the memory. The hammocks were not very comfortable, but they had definitely provided an entertainment factor that could not be beat. Between Galena and Morgo, he'd laughed more in the last couple of days than he had in weeks. "Can you show me Morak? He and a group of his archers left yesterday morning sometime and I haven't heard back from them, not that I really expected to. I just want to make sure nothing has happened to them."

Nodding, Morgo retrieved his bowl from where he flung it and sat in a chair next to Tark so they could both see. Within seconds, the image of Morak appeared in the bowl. He seemed to be crouching down with another elf. They were watching something from their hiding place. Other than looking like they were being cautious, which Tark appreciated, they appeared to be fine.

"I wish we could see where they are," Tark commented as he continued to watch Morak peeking through the brush.

"That might be something for Galena to try. This type of viewing takes a great deal of concentration and that's just with watching one subject. When we try to back up and take in other aspects, normal elves will burn out too quickly to gather that much information. But this may not apply to Galena seeing how most of the rules I have had to live by haven't applied to her," Morgo replied.

"This is true," Tark said thoughtfully. "Are you going to continue spending time with Venia should we survive this?" Tark asked. He looked at the ground, giving Morgo a chance to collect his thoughts.

"Would it be offensive if I did?" Morgo asked slowly in response to this.

"What if she does come out of this sort of trance she's in and she doesn't reciprocate your feelings?"

"I guess that's a chance I have to be willing to take." Morgo looked slightly crestfallen at this, but snapped out of it quickly. "I assume you're going to go see Galena now?"

Tark was surprised at the abrupt change of subject, but after getting to know Morgo, took the shift in stride. "I hadn't actually thought about it, but if I want to find out if she can see the whereabouts of Morak and Rau's army, I probably should take a stroll over to visit her. I'll head there now, seeing how she normally wakes early."

"Would you mind if I tagged along? I am curious to see if my theory was correct."

"You're always curious about something."

"Indeed, it's how we learn. Shall we go?"

"If you're ready." Morgo indicated the open tent with a sweep of his arm.

Grinning, Tark stood and headed out to see his sister. "Do you think we even have a chance of winning?" Tark asked quietly as they covered the ground between Morgo's tent and Galena's. The question plagued him since they started on this quest and after seeing less than half of Rau's army, he felt his fears were confirmed.

"That's an interesting question," Morgo said thoughtfully. "On the one hand, Rau has us hopelessly outnumbered. On the other hand, we have magical abilities the dark creatures will never have. So it is brute strength against magic, which cancels each other out. So then we're left with the question, who wants to win more, the elves or Rau?"

Tark had never thought of it that way. Morgo certainly had an interesting way of looking at things. He had never failed to amuse Tark with his theories.

"Do you think it will boil down to Galena versus Rau too?"

"I most certainly do. How else would it all end?" Morgo said, looking at Tark curiously.

"Good point."

They saw Galena slipping through the tent entrance when they drew close to her tent. Tark had to smile, he knew her so well. "Galena, wait."

Galena stopped and turned to face them, a look of surprise on her face. "What are you two doing up so early?" she called out when they had almost reached her.

"We would like to try an experiment, if you would humor us," Morgo said, smiling at her.

"What kind of experiment did you have in mind?" she asked a little cautiously.

"It won't kill you, if that's what you're worried about," Tark said good-humoredly.

Galena shook her head. She appeared to be unsure of what to think of this last statement.

"That makes me feel so much better," she mumbled.

"Shall we head back to my tent, since I assume by your quiet exit, Elenio is still asleep?"

"Sure." The trio headed back in the direction from which Morgo and Tark came. When they reached the tent, Morgo retrieved his mirror water bowl and handed it to Galena. "We already know I can see images in water," Galena said, a bemused look on her face.

"Yes, but now we want to see if you can see the surroundings of your main focus," Morgo said, filling the bowl with water as he explained what they wanted.

"How do I do that?" Galena asked.

"I'm not entirely sure as I have never been able to accomplish that particular task. I assume it's a lot like viewing an image and then directing or thinking of yourself zooming back so that you can see the things surrounding that image. This is just an assumption and those can often be wrong. I only know an elf with a normal amount of magic cannot accomplish this goal because of the amount of power and concentration it takes. Not all elves can bring a single image up in the mirror waters. It's like I mentioned before, some elves can do some types of magic and other elves can accomplish other things. You are the only exception to this rule."

"Okay, now that this has been explained so it's as clear as mud, let's give it a whirl," Galena said sarcastically while looking into the bowl of water. "What am I looking for?"

"We want to see where Rau's army is first off and then if you could bring up Morak and the rest of his archers that would help too," Tark said. He watched the images swirling around in the water, waiting for Galena to direct them into clearer focus.

Galena nodded and stared intently at the water, the images it held becoming sharper with each moment. There in the waters were the thousands of dark creatures remaining in the army Rau sent out. They appeared to be on the move, but as to where they were at, they would only be able to know if this experiment worked.

"Now, imagine you are flying away from them, higher into the air," Morgo whispered, his attention too was on the images within the water. Instantly, the creatures began to shrink and more came into view. It took a lot longer than Tark would have imagined for Galena to get high enough to view more than the dark creatures. Finally, they were able to identify the region through which the army moved.

"They are moving at an incredible pace," Morgo noted thoughtfully, his gaze still intent on the scene.

"Rau must have told them to get there quickly, or they're afraid of you. I'm curious to know the reason behind their break neck pace," Tark said, taking his eyes off the mirror waters and sitting back in one of the chairs.

Galena blinked her eyes several times, causing the images to disappear. Returning her gaze on the waters, she thought of Morak and instantly saw him in the water. They appeared to be right behind the army, but still at enough of a distance that they were safe. Galena cleared the image away along with the water and then placed the empty bowl on the ground beside Morgo's hammock. She sat down gingerly, looking somewhat tired after the experiment.

"So they're roughly four days ahead of us," she said after a bit.

"So it seems," Tark replied.

"And you still don't think we need to get started sooner?"

"No, I don't. I think you need to give yourself a bit more time and we have other magical elves that need the rest. You're not the only important one," Tark said, grinning in an amused way.

Galena sighed heavily and stood. "Well, if you two are through experimenting with me, I'm off to find some food and rest up since it's so necessary."

"Galena, we'll head out tomorrow morning at first light."

"By then, they'll be a week ahead of us."

"Then so be it."

Chapter Seven

Galena knew deep down Tark was being reasonable, but she felt they were somehow wasting time by not starting after Rau's army. Even if they didn't catch up within a couple of days, they would at least keep them from getting so far ahead. She stormed in the direction she smelled food, hoping to find some sweet bread there. She managed to lose the crumbs she had been using to make more of it on their return trip. She assumed this happened when she tossed her bag down.

Elenio had retrieved her bag when she'd been recovering from her big battle and to her immense relief, Twoit stayed with the pack during the battle. Elenio said she appeared to have been asleep the entire time. Since the arrival to camp however, she made herself scarce just as she had done with the other camps. Apparently, the ferret had aversions to elves other than Galena and her companions, which suited Galena fine. She'd only seen the ferret once in the last couple of days and that was when Twoit was sneaking back into the tent after hunting the night before. Earlier that morning, she noticed the tiny creature had curled up at the foot of the hammock and slept the night away with Galena without her knowing.

Galena knew she'd arrived at the right tent because the smells of good things to eat were stronger here. Galena's stomach gave a loud rumble and much to her embarrassment, the elf who was entering the tent next to her chuckled as they passed. *Yeah, yeah, I know,* she thought to herself.

Inside, she found several elves sitting on the ground, their hands full of food. Galena took a deep breath of the warm smells of bread and sweet smells of fruit, her mouth salivating in response. She entered and stopped in shock when all the elves in the tent, stood and bowed low to her before they began clapping. Galena felt more than a little uncomfortable at the sight of so many elves treating her like royalty. She'd been here a couple of days and all the elves she passed while in camp had thanked her personally, but this was the first time this many responded to her at once. It was overwhelming.

"Please, you are to be thanked as much as I," she said loudly while she held her hands up to quiet them. "What I do, I am doing for you and for those we left behind. Please, do not thank me for the gift I've been given. I don't deserve it."

The elves responded by bowing low once more as a sign of respect before sitting down to finish their food. Galena approached the area where she could get a variety of different things to eat and chose a loaf of sweet bread, several pieces of cheese, fruits, and vegetables. Not only her hands were full, but so were her arms. Even then, she realized she would have to use the wind to help her carry it all. One of the underground elves who was in charge of the food, laughed at her when she saw the burden she carried.

"We won't run out," she said, laughing.

Galena blushed. She nodded in thanks and set off for her tent once more. If she thought she had attracted attention before, it was nothing compared to the stares she now received. Every elf that passed did a double take causing Galena's face to turn redder with every glance. Finally, she reached the safety of her tent, where no eyes could follow her and the large amount of food she carried.

"Hungry?" Elenio asked, laughing when Galena entered the tent.

"Yes, but I brought some for you too," Galena said indignantly.

"Well, you never know with you," Elenio said, smiling broadly.

Galena rolled her eyes at this and handed him several pieces of food. Elenio kept his eyes on her at all times, the smile never leaving his lips.

"Where were you off to, besides hoarding half of the elves' rations?"

That does it, she thought. She'd had enough of the teasing. Using the wind, she sent a small chunk of bread flying through the air and straight up Elenio's nose, where it lodged nicely.

Elenio's smile disappeared from his face as the discomfort of having food shoved up his nostril replaced his amusement. He choked and began to sneeze furiously before he closed his other nostril with a finger. With a mighty effort, he blew the chunk of bread out and sent it bouncing across the floor. Galena roared with laughter throughout the entire process, tears streaming down her face when he was finally able to dislodge the food. Elenio studiously ignored Galena through the remainder of their morning meal, for which Galena was perfectly fine with, now that she felt better.

"Tark and Morgo had me do a sort of experiment this morning."

Still attempting to ignore Galena, Elenio continued to eat, but Galena could tell she had gotten his attention when he turned his face so he could hear her better.

She smiled before continuing. "They wanted to see if I would be able to see the landscape surrounding Rau's army. I was successful. Unfortunately, we found out they're already several days ahead of us. The ridiculous part is that Tark is still maintaining we need to wait until tomorrow morning before we head out."

"I agree with him."

"Somehow, I knew that was what you were going to say," Galena grumbled.

"Galena, have you even talked to any of the other underground elves besides Nigora?"

Galena looked at Elenio, waiting for him to continue.

"Nigora wasn't the only one who was passed out by the end of the day. Morgo and I went around checking on the other magical elves. They were all passed out. Only Nina actually made it to her hammock. The others were found near their tents or passing elves took pity on them and placed them in their tents. Most of them, I imagine, still have not stirred from where they lay. Tark told me when they began to use their magic to build tree homes a good many of them would be out for days at a time. He also said they had gotten better over the weeks, but big and different magic is still hard on them. Now, in order for us to get into Blackwell, we need every elf we can spare. So quit complaining and accept we need to give others a chance to catch up."

Galena felt stunned. Elenio had never been so blunt with her before.

"So, what you're saying is that you really don't like bread up your nose?"

65

Elenio looked at her in shock, before abruptly getting up and storming out of the tent.

Well, that didn't go quite like I was hoping, Galena thought miserably. Getting up, she ran out after Elenio who was storming off in the direction of Tark and Taura's tent. "Elenio, wait!" she called out to him.

He stopped, but refused to turn around.

"I'm sorry. I don't know what's gotten into me."

He acknowledged her by turning to face her as she continued.

"Chalk it up to feeling like I have been laughed at more often by more elves and feeling completely helpless. I shouldn't have gotten upset either with you or Tark. I know you're both right, I just hate to admit it."

Elenio's face softened when she finished and grabbing her hand, he pulled her to him where he could wrap his arms around her. "I'm sorry too," he muttered into her hair, kissing the top of her head. "I didn't mean to be so blunt earlier, I just felt like I was dealing with a two year old." He tickled Galena's side causing her to wriggle around, fighting to get away from the torturous fingers. He stopped and pulled her close to him once more. "That and I got used to having you all to myself. I don't like having to share you with everyone and I really don't like the fact that if it hadn't been for you, we would still be fighting."

"Elenio…" Galena started, but Elenio stopped her by placing a hand over her mouth.

"I wasn't finished yet," he said, putting a finger under her chin and raising her face so she was looking directly at him.

She saw weariness there, hidden in the circles around his eyes and the tightness around his mouth. She knew he had been through as much as she had and would have to go through much more before they were finished.

He kissed her nose and resting his forehead on hers he continued, "I'm getting better, but there is some male instinct there that tells me I'm the one that is supposed to be protecting you, not the other way around. No matter how many battles we go through or how many tight situations you get me out of, that instinct is always going to be there. Just ask Tark, Morgo, and Morak. They will tell you the same thing holds true for them as well. So be patient with me for it will always be a struggle and one that my better judgment will not always win." He smiled at this last statement before kissing her quickly.

Galena smiled in return and took a step back. "Shall we head to Tark's and see what the plan is for tomorrow?"

Elenio nodded his head in response before taking Galena's hand once more and starting in the direction that he had been heading.

Galena felt better after settling their argument. After all that they had been through, it seemed silly to go on being angry at one another for sheer pettiness.

Within a few moments, they arrived at Tark's tent to find Taura alone. After giving them both a hug, she told them Tark started out early that morning and she hadn't seen him since the night before. She also said he could normally be found with one of his generals. They thanked her and headed out to Morgo's tent, but found that neither of them were there. Finally, after they ran into Hasa, they were able to meet up with Tark who was indeed meeting with Fala, Morgo, Nina, and Naradin on different battle tactics and their overall impression about the first attempt. Galena threw in her two cents while Elenio sat back and listened to it all. Naradin felt that they might do better if they surrounded Rau's army, but Tark laughed this idea away.

"We don't even have enough elves to surround one side, let alone all of them."

Naradin looked grim at this reminder and thoughtfully sat back.

"The earlier we leave, the better. I think we should pick off as many as possible before they reach Blackwell. Once they do, it will be nearly impossible to gain any ground," Elenio said thoughtfully.

"Galena could always blast her way through," Nina said sarcastically, but this remark was met with Elenio and Tark's instant disapproval.

Morgo held up a hand to silence their further complaints before saying, "She only teases. You forget we know better than any other elves how far you can take magic. However, you do realize it will take something of Galena size to finally get to Rau." Morgo was staring at the floor at this last statement while he waited for everyone to absorb what he told them.

"As much as I would like to say no, I realize that would be fool hardy," Tark nearly whispered.

"So, I guess the real question is how do you plan to get into Blackwell, Galena?" Morgo asked, still looking at the floor.

All eyes turned to look at Galena, but she found that she couldn't meet any of them, especially not Elenio's or Tark's. "Ummm, I hadn't thought that far, but I definitely plan on doing something to keep us from dying," Galena muttered to no one in particular.

"Spoken like a true hero," Elenio said, rolling his eyes as he did.

"Well, it's definitely a start," Morgo said grinning broadly at Galena. "I've got a couple ideas on the matter."

"Sounds like a plan," Galena said, returning Morgo's grin.

"It definitely sounds like I've thought of it a bit more than you have," Morgo said, chuckling as he did.

"You think about everything more than anyone else!" Tark exclaimed.

Chapter Eight

True to his word, Tark had the entire camp packed and ready to go before the sun ceased to touch the land in the far distance. The tents and all the hammocks were stowed away in a single pack with a magical trick Morgo showed Galena when they were traveling through the tunnels of the underground world such a very long time ago. She shrunk everything to the size of an ant. Morgo told her it took all the underground elves to pack, unpack, and construct the entire camp. Even then, they hadn't been able to do it all at once, but had to resort to doing a handful of tents at a time so they could preserve their energy. It took them a little over an hour to do what Galena did in a matter of minutes with energy to spare.

Galena spent most of the morning walking beside Morgo and discussing the different strategies he thought would prove beneficial when it came to battling Rau or even how to get to him. They were both sure he would place every dark creature both named and unnamed between himself and Galena. He wouldn't risk going directly against her until she forced his hand. Many of the ideas revolved around trying to use lightning or something else big to create an opening, but Galena felt this would be equivalent to Morgo trying to put creature after creature to sleep, eventually she would wear out.

Throughout Morgo and her discussions, Elenio walked patiently beside Galena, listening intently and offering suggestions at random. He never openly said it, but Galena could feel the fear radiate in him for her. She felt bad for him, knowing exactly how he felt because of her experience in that horrible cave. She reached out and taking his hand, gave it a squeeze, trying to reassure him, but knowing it was useless to try. No one would rest easy until the war was finished. Even then, if

Galena lost, the elves left would have to go into hiding. She wasn't sure what Elenio would do and tried not to think of it.

The elves walked through the entire day and only stopped to rest and eat late that night. The following day, like the morning before, they set out before sunrise once more. Tark had Galena check on the progress of the dark creatures and found they'd stopped just a short distance away from Blackwell. They appeared to have set up camp. Now they were waiting for the elves to make their appearance. Galena also searched for Morak and found him and his elves heading in the opposite direction of the enemy's camp. They were jogging at an even pace and making good time. Tark figured if the elves kept traveling as well as they had and Morak's group kept traveling at the pace they were, the two groups would meet within a couple of days.

Once again, the elves moved out as soon as the sun peeked above the distant land. This time they didn't have to worry about packing up because they had all slept under the stars. They traveled in this manner for roughly a week, meeting up with Morak and his group on the third day as Tark predicted. It was on the seventh day when they came within seeing distance of the enemy's camp. Galena could smell the salty sea on the breeze. She had never been this far south in the land of Tomiro. The Mountains of the Gods had been the farthest she'd ever been and even then, they didn't lie on the outer edges of land, but more in the general southern part.

Blackwell was on a small island a short way from the southernmost point of Tomiro. Galena had always heard stories of how dark and depressing the land was in that region, but hadn't realized how much so until she had reached it. Death and darkness was the most prominent feature in this forsaken land. The sky above even gave up trying to fight the dark of Blackwell and had the permanent look of an approaching thunderstorm. The ground below as far as the eye could see was varying shades of black and gray. The dark intunerics were scattered all throughout the area and were said to make up the very walls of Blackwell. They had sucked the surrounding land dry of anything good and containing life. *Very long here and we won't have to battle Rau, the stones will kill us,* Galena thought dryly.

"We'll make camp here tonight and tomorrow we'll engage the enemy," Tark said with a look of determination and disgust on his face. "Make sure everyone at least has a hammock to sleep on. I want no one lying on this ground for any length of time. They may not wake up if they do."

The generals nodded their heads in agreement and set off to inform all of the elves of their plans.

"Kind of feels like we've arrived at death's door, doesn't it?" Elenio said, eyeing the enemy army and the surrounding land with disdain.

Galena said nothing to this, but looked at the enemy as well. They seemed much more intimidating surrounded by all the dark and gloom. Perhaps it was because they blended in so well with the surroundings, it made them appear to have doubled in size. It was possible Rau may have sent reinforcements, although Galena somehow doubted this because she felt he was truly a coward at heart and wanted his strongest closest to him.

"Come on, let's help set up some hammocks. I have a feeling sleep will not come easy in this place," Galena said, shuddering slightly at the thought of trying to fall asleep in a land that seemed filled with nightmares. If any land needed light in it, it was this one.

The next morning was as dark and gloomy as the day before. The only reason Galena knew it was day was because the night had been the darkest Galena had ever been through. Without the aid of lanterns or campfire, she had not been able see her hand in front of her face. Elenio still claimed she glowed faintly, but she couldn't see it. The chill that had seeped into her very bones, made her feel depressed and alone. She could tell by Elenio's thoughts and emotions that he felt the same.

She awoke and waking Elenio, because she refused to be apart from him for even a moment since they had arrived, they went to find Tark. They found him, along with several of his generals, going over last minute instructions before setting off to meet the enemy. Galena looked over at Morgo who looked as tired as she felt.

"Rough night too?" she asked, looking concerned.

"I was haunted by nightmare after nightmare. It seemed as soon as I would wake from one, another would follow. All my worst fears placed in my dreams to torture me."

71

Not for the first time was Galena thankful Mira had taken her ability to dream from her. She could only imagine what the night would have held for her if she hadn't.

"Tell me about it," Elenio said darkly.

"I think that was the common theme for the night," Tark said, joining them. "Were you able to sleep at all?" he asked, looking at Galena, worry coloring his voice.

"My dreams were taken from me. A blessing from Mira," Galena answered as she looked in the direction of the dark army. "When are we heading out?"

"Within the hour," Tark answered. He turned to look at the enemy army as Galena was. "Why?"

"I'm going to see who would like to own a blazing blade," Galena said, smiling at Tark as she did.

"Glad you can find something amusing in all this mess." Tark shook his head in amazement as Galena continued to grin mischievously.

"Giving us an advantage should make everyone happy."

"Just make sure that they understand the spell will react anytime the sword comes in contact with any living flesh. It doesn't matter if the flesh belongs to good or evil," Morgo said, coming up on the other side of Tark.

"Got it. Care to come with me to help explain the rules and provide water for the ones who manage to set themselves ablaze for not following those rules?" Galena asked.

"Lead the way," Morgo said.

"Elenio, are you coming?"

"No, I want to talk with Tark for a little while. I'll catch up in a bit." He too was staring in the direction of the enemy army, a look of disgust on his face.

Galena looked at him for a moment more, debating whether she wanted to argue about this, but decided against it. Instead, she turned and followed Morgo, who was already heading to a group of elves preparing for battle.

Galena and Morgo had talked to several groups of elves and put spells on most of their weapons, when Elenio finally caught up with them. He looked grim, but stood back and watched as Morgo explained to another group the idea of having blazing weapons. Galena backed up, knowing Morgo would be able to do a much better job convincing the elves than she would and turned to Elenio.

"What was that about?" she asked so only he would be able to hear. She felt a sadness wash over him and thoughts of her battling the enemy army alone as she had before flashed through his mind. "Oh."

"I'm not saying anything or trying to convince you to do differently," he said, watching as several elves in the group stepped forward to have spells put on their arrows and swords. "It's not my fault you know my thoughts." He looked back at her and grinned halfheartedly.

"I love you. Would you like me to blindfold you or tie you up so you don't have to watch?" Galena asked, smiling and poking him in the side.

"Yeah, because tying me up worked so well before." He raised his tunic sleeve showing her the scars left from wrestling with a vine. When she had been in the cave fighting against the fears of her mind, Elenio had been struggling with a vine the guardian tied him to a tree with in order to keep him from attempting to get into the cave and saving her. When Galena emerged from the depths of the darkness contained within the vanishing mountain, she needed to heal all the cuts and bruises on Elenio, but some of the deeper cuts had left ragged scars on his arms for which she could do nothing about.

"True, so maybe I'll keep you locked up in a giant air bubble."

Elenio looked at her curiously and Galena saw flashes of his thoughts race through his mind.

"Interesting," she said as she pieced together the thoughts. "It might be worth a try once we decide we need a break." Morgo was finishing up with the explanations, which meant that Galena was up.

She fixed the fire within each of the weapons and turned back to Elenio when Morgo shouted. She rolled her eyes, extinguishing yet another elf with a wave of her hands. *Apparently, not all the elves listened carefully,* she thought. Fortunately, for the elf, no serious damage had been done other than the burn marks on his pants. *Maybe this wasn't such a good idea.*

* * * *

The elves gathered and stood waiting a short distance from the dark creatures Rau sent out. Unlike the first battle, there was nothing but flat, dark land all around. There were no good hiding places for the archers to shoot from, so Tark settled for keeping them toward the back of the elf army. He briefly considered placing them on some of the larger intunerics, but it made the elves feel drained when they stood on them for too long. This suited Galena fine, she had an idea that involved their use.

Galena stood at the front of their army with Elenio and Morgo on one side, Tark and Taura on the other. The other generals were placed strategically throughout the remaining forces surrounded by those they trained. She felt sick at the thought of what was to come, knowing this was just another step toward Rau. Regardless of what she let the others think, she was terrified with the idea of fighting the darkest creature in all of Tomiro. She knew she had no other choice, but it didn't help her to feel less afraid.

She knew the elves killed several dark creatures the last time. She, herself, had taken on several hundred and destroyed all of them. However, when she looked at the readying army before her, it seemed as if they hadn't even put a dent in the rolling mass of darkness. *How discouraging,* she thought. *To think there were more waiting for them at Blackwell, including the vicious and frightening Tookoos.* She shuddered involuntarily as she thought of those dreaded creatures. They made the earagos seem tame in comparison.

Elenio reached for her hand, giving it a comforting squeeze, sensing her thoughts and fears. She tried to smile at him reassuringly, but only managed to pull off a grimace. He, however, smiled at her efforts before turning back to look at the growing mass of darkness in front of them. It seemed to swell in size, doing nothing to calm Galena's anxieties.

"I don't know about you guys, but I get the impression they're trying to intimidate us," Morgo said sarcastically.

"If you're referring to their looks, then that's not intimidation, they've always been that ugly," Tark replied, feigning a calm Galena knew none of them felt, but she had to smile at his attempt at humor during this time. She saw Taura roll her eyes and shake her head at her commitment partner's remark, making Galena's smile widen even more.

No matter what, she would protect her family and friends with her every breath. She couldn't watch them die again. She wasn't strong enough.

"What do you say about not giving them a chance to attack first this time? Let's give them a greeting they'll be sure to remember. Galena, would you mind giving Morak the signal?" Tark asked, watching the dark creatures ahead of him preparing themselves for battle by removing their blades and clubs from around their waists.

Galena raised her hand and shot a column of fire straight into the air. As they planned, a torrent of arrows flew over the heads of the elves and into the crowd of dark creatures, catching fire as soon as they encountered any flesh. The result was a large number of the enemy front lines were now dancing around in flames.

"Well, I think we got their attention," Elenio said, readying his sword as the enemy took the fire arrows as the signal they should attack.

"Yep, that definitely did the trick," Tark answered back.

The first of the torlics came charging at them, blades ready. It had an evil grin on his bright, red face, his long, black hair streaming behind him like a flag, encouraging others on.

Leaping into the air, Galena met him head on, striking his blade with her own. The familiar energy of the sword coursed through her body, giving her a rush like no other. The torlic pulled his blade back and swinging around, he meant to cut into Galena's side, but she deflected the blow easily. She spun around and aiming low, cutting deep into the monster's leg. Like so many other dark creatures that felt the kiss of the Sword of Lumina, he burst into pieces, light replacing the dark. She turned to meet another one as he swung his sword down and toward her head. She blocked the blow and returned one, stabbing him in the belly, and causing him to erupt into blinding light as well.

From the corner of her eye, she saw both Tark and Taura handling an earagos, alternating swings until they brought the giant to its knees where Tark landed the final blow. She smiled while fending herself from three torlics and a narooks. The narooks tried to wrap its fingers around her neck, but only succeeded in losing his fingers before succumbing to the death the Sword of Lumina held for every dark creature. She made quick work of two of the torlics while Elenio dispatched of the third, causing it to catch flame as his sword met the torlics skin.

"I really like having a sword with fire," he said grinning broadly.

"Let me know when you need a recharge," Galena shouted, while she took down one of the two dark creatures for which she had no name. They reminded her somewhat of a cross between a narooks and a torlic, with the wings of a Crag. Not a very appealing mix in her mind.

Elenio swung around, burying his blade deep into the side of a narooks before spinning around and cutting one of the wings off the creature that Galena was fighting. Both creatures caught fire before he turned around to assist Morgo with an earagos he saw heading their way.

Galena turned to take on a rather small earagos single-handedly. She jabbed her blade down, catching the giant in the foot and destroying it with light. Tark was fighting against a group of narooks while taura fought against two torlics, both seemed to be holding their own. Galena noted they were covered in blood, but none of it seemed to be theirs, rather it belonged to the creatures with which they fought.

Galena turned to take in the condition of the other elves surrounding them, flying off the ones who were lying on the ground injured, in the general direction of Nigora's tent. She'd managed to land them safely when a group of torlics surrounded her, thinking she was occupied. *Silly creatures,* she thought, *haven't you learned anything?* She spun around meeting blade after blade with her own sword. She swung out and the wind took two of them, sent them high into the air and several hundred feet away before they dropped on the ground in giant heaps. Two more she struck with lightning, and while the others were distracted, she swung her blade around burying it in the back of one and the side of the other, both became pieces that were scattered in the wind. She was about to engage several more dark creatures when she heard a sound that caused her blood to turn to ice in her veins.

"GALENA! HELP!" she heard Elenio shout from somewhere behind her. Wasting no time with the creatures around her, she set them all ablaze before she searched for Elenio. She found him on the shoulders of a giant earagos. It was larger than any of the earagos she'd seen so far. He was cutting at its back with no effect on the giant creature whatsoever. Galena then looked down and saw what was keeping the earagos so focused. Below him, on the ground in a bloody heap, was

Morgo. The earagos was hitting him repeatedly with its giant club, making his body even more unrecognizable.

"ELENIO, MOVE!" she shouted as she raced over to him. Elenio jumped from the back of the creature and with a wave of her hand, she sent the earagos flying into the air and into another earagos some feet away. She watched as the culprit got shakily to his feet, shaking his head as he did. She would deal with him in a moment. She raced to Morgo's side. His legs were at an odd angle and he definitely shouldn't have been able to bend that way. His face was unrecognizable under the swelling and blood that seemed to cover every inch of his once handsome features. He had a large gap at the crown of his skull; his blade lay uselessly beside him. Galena leaned her ear close to his face and was surprised to hear a faint, raspy breath. It was shallow and almost nonexistent, but it was there.

"I'll take him to Nigora," Fala said above her.

"You hold him and I'll fly you back. I don't trust myself to land him gently enough when he's this bad. I'll be there as soon as I can. He is beyond what Nigora can do for him," Galena said darkly.

"We could all use a break at this point. They're driving us back. It's almost like they're stronger here with the intunerics feeding them," Tark said, panting heavily. He had come over as well to fend off any attacking creatures with Elenio and Taura while Galena had looked at Morgo.

Galena nodded her head and turned to Fala.

"Are you ready?" she asked.

Fala scooped up the broken form of Morgo, causing his head to roll in a revolting sort of way. Blood streamed to the ground from gashes unseen, causing the already pale elf to become deathly gray.

Galena had to choke back a sob at the broken form of Morgo, unsure if she would ever see him alive again. "I'll be with you as soon as I can, just hang on," she whispered into his ear, unsure if he was past the point where he could no longer hear her. Picking Fala and Morgo up with a gentle wind, she sent them flying at a controlled speed until she was sure they were somewhere near Nigora's tent. Wiping the tears from her eyes, she turned back and looked at the approaching enemy. They were indeed pushing the elves back at an alarming speed. More elf bodies littered the ground than those of the enemy, a sure sign they needed to regroup.

"Time to put our plan into action," Galena shouted, more tears springing to her eyes, as it had been Morgo's plan originally. "Mira be with him," she prayed quietly. Sending another column of flames high into the air, all the elves began to race toward the camp, grabbing their fallen comrades as they did. The enemy started to give chase as well, but Galena discouraged this with a couple well-aimed lightning bolts. When she saw all of the elves had retreated toward their camp, Galena decided to use the intunerics to their advantage. Using the wind to pick up every stone within a mile of the elf camp, she lifted them into the air and sent them flying into the enemy army. She heard the satisfying sound of dull thuds and groans of pain resonate from within the dark mass. *There you go, plenty of dark rocks to play with,* Galena thought grimly.

"Now, time to give us a little breathing space," she whispered aloud. Concentrating on the elf camp and all the elves within that area, she sent a blazing, white-hot ring of fire around her and everyone she loved. She caused the ring of fire to grow higher and higher until even the tallest earagos could no longer see over it. She waited to see if it would hold should any of the dark creatures be foolish enough to try crossing the barrier. They did not disappoint her. Several torlics and even more narooks thought they would be able to race across the fire ring, but Galena already thought they would try this and took measures for just that occasion. As soon as the dark creatures touched the flames, it burned even hotter and grew wider in response, causing the dark creature to catch fire. The creature was not able to return from which it came before falling to the ground, food for the living barrier. More tears streamed down her face, Morgo's idea worked perfectly.

She caused the wind to lift her up high into the air where she could see the enemy army above the fire. She saw the earagos that had broken and possibly even killed her friend, grin evilly at her. He seemed to realize how much damage he did and reveled in his accomplishment. He even had enough nerve to wave at Galena, rubbing in his victory. Galena's blood boiled, and anger filled her. *Think this is over do you,* she thought, her ears ringing with the blood that so violently rushed through her. "Wrong," she whispered aloud.

A giant bolt of lightning, larger than anything she caused so far, came racing to the ground and into the head of the waving earagos, stopping him in mid wave. A smile still frozen on his ugly face, he crashed to the ground, dead. "That was for Morgo," she said angrily. Turning, she sent herself flying toward Nigora's tent to see what had become of her friend and mentor.

* * * *

Elenio grabbed a female elf with a deep cut on her leg, but otherwise appeared to be fine. He knew they were to grab any fallen elves on the way back to the camp as they were instructed the day before, but he was in a hurry to see Morgo. It had been his fault his friend was struck in the first place. Elenio hadn't been paying attention to anything around him as he delivered the deathblow to the first earagos they met. So when he turned to say something witty to Morgo, he was surprised to see another even larger earagos standing over him, his club poised to strike.

Elenio had no time to prepare himself when the giant beast's arm started down. Elenio remembered feeling as if he was flying when Morgo crashed into him, pushing him out of the way, and putting himself into position to take the blow instead. The club came down squarely on Morgo's head, causing him to crumple to the ground, unmoving. As if that hadn't been enough, this particular earagos seemed to have an incredibly vicious streak and continued to beat the unconscious elf. That was when Elenio had called out to Galena and jumped on the broad back of the evil creature. Elenio thought, if he could just hurt the giant brute bad enough, it would give up its assault on Morgo and turn his attention to Elenio, who was in much better shape to defend himself. Fortunately, that was when Galena showed up and at least gotten the creature away from Morgo. Elenio was unsure what had become of the earagos after Galena had sent him flying. He secretly hoped he would have the chance to exact some revenge on the brute.

Elenio drew near Nigora's healing tent, his heart sinking when he saw all the elves injured and in need of attention. However, that was not the reason Elenio felt sick. Blood, soaking into the ground around the entrance, covering the tent flap, it was everywhere Elenio looked. He swallowed and then lowered the female to the ground gently so he wouldn't hurt her further. She grimaced, but nodded her head in thanks before laying back on the ground to await her turn with the healer.

Elenio stood straight and squaring his shoulders, stepped through the tent flap and into Nigora's domain. The devastation that consumed the inside of that tent was overwhelming. There were injured elves everywhere, but it was a closed off area that caught Elenio's attention. Behind it, he could just make out the tall and imposing frame of Fala. Tark came in about that time and Elenio met his gaze with his own.

"Has Galena put up the fire barrier?" he asked dully.

"Yes, she's doing something at the battlegrounds right now, but I'm sure she'll be on her way in a moment," Tark answered quietly. They both made their ways toward the closed off area, weaving between beds and other elves.

"Is Taura okay?" Elenio asked, trying to keep his mind off what they were about to encounter.

"She's fine. She outside trying to do what she can for some of the injured elves while they wait. We have more injured this time in that short battle then we did the entire time we fought the last time. I think the intunerics had something to do with it, but I can't be sure," Tark said, his brows burrowed in concern.

Elenio pulled back the sheet used to close off the area where Morgo lay and stepped through. What he saw didn't leave him with much hope for his friend. Nigora was sitting in a chair beside him, heavily slumped to one side. Her face covered in sweat and she was a shade of gray that caused Elenio to bend down and check her pulse. He was relieved to find one, but realized her unconscious state spoke badly for Morgo.

Morgo was lying on a table. His legs straightened out, but still looked wrong. The gap at the top of his head was closed, which was good because that was where he lost the most blood. His face was still unrecognizable under the swelling, dirt, and blood. There were slits where his eyes should have been and his nose was flush with his cheekbones. His side sunk in at a weird angle and there were bones sticking out from the other. His chest barely rose and fell, but he was still breathing. Elenio had no idea how this was possible and almost wished his friend would pass on to the Land of the Gods versus being in this state.

"Nigora managed to close up the wound on his head before she passed out. She said there was a tremendous amount of brain damage there because of the swelling and other trauma…" Fala started, but he stopped to clear his throat. "She didn't have a lot of hope for him. She said there was entirely too much internal and external damage for anyone to have survived. The fact he's still breathing is a miracle." Fala stopped and looked down at the ground, tears in his eyes.

Elenio just looked at his friend, thanking him silently for saving his own life, but wishing at the same time, he hadn't.

"Galena is coming," Tark said dully, looking up and down at the broken form of Morgo.

"Do you really think she'll be able to reverse all of this?" Fala asked, using a hand to indicate the form that they once knew as Morgo.

"She can try."

"Then she better hurry, because I'm pretty sure no one can bring an elf back from the Land of the Gods."

Elenio could do nothing but stare. It was his fault. Why hadn't he been paying attention?

"Leave." All three of the elves turned to see Galena there, holding back the sheet as she took in the bloody image of Morgo. Her eyes were sad as she noted every injury on her friend. "Take Nigora, she needs to rest. Start making the other elves as comfortable as possible and we need patrols circling the camp to make sure my fire holds out the enemies," Galena said, her eyes never leaving Morgo for a second.

"Can you…" Elenio started, but stopped when his throat closed up with emotion.

Galena looked at him, determination filling her eyes as she read his thoughts and emotions.

"I don't know. I know he would never let you take the blame."

Tears sprang to Elenio's eyes and he couldn't speak. He knew she read his thoughts and he realized she was right, but it didn't make him feel any better.

"I already killed the brute," Galena spat having registered his own thoughts of revenge. "He thought he won. I showed him just how wrong he was."

Galena's focus returned to Morgo and Elenio nodded his head, glad the creature was gone, but sorry he couldn't have been a bigger part in his demise.

"Now everyone leave and do not bother me. I will come to you one way or the other," Galena finished lamely.

Fala picked up the tiny form of Nigora in his strong capable arms and with Tark holding the sheet back, went out with her. Tark followed him and Elenio brought up the rear. He knew Galena needed to be able to concentrate. He didn't think he would be able to sit back and wait to see the fate of his friend. Tark reached over and squeezed Elenio's shoulder, but said nothing. They both knew this would be exactly like their trip to the Mountains of the Gods. Morgo's fate rested with them now.

* * * *

Galena took a step closer to Morgo. If she hadn't been told this was him, she would have doubted it and went looking for the elf elsewhere. The only thing resembling her friend was his long, dark hair. Although, now it was matted and caked with dried blood. She leaned her ear close to his mouth and felt as well as heard the faint and weak breath there. A gurgling sound came with it, leading Galena to believe his lungs were punctured. *How could they not be,"* Galena thought, eyeing the broken body. She cut away his shirt, reveling the grossly discolored and swollen chest. Bits of bone punctured the skin and it rose and fell in odd areas as well.

"Oh Morgo, I don't know if it's wise to heal you if you're this bad off," Galena said through the tears falling fast and free down her face. Galena laid her hands on Morgo's rib cage and began the tedious task of sensing the overwhelming amount of injuries fighting against his will to live. She detected punctures to his lungs in several place and his heart was a battered mess. Not a single organ in his body escaped the wrath of the earagos. She placed a hand on his head and felt the extensive damage there as well. His brain was bruised and shaken loose, making it useless in its present condition. There was also extensive bleeding there, held in by the newly healed gap. There wasn't a whole bone in his body. Galena bowed her head, and fought to regain control of her emotions. She reached out, seeking Elenio, for she would need his calm if she were to continue. She felt Elenio and knew he was striving to find the peace she needed. She took a calming breath and began.

Chapter Nine

Tark sat back on the ground, tired beyond belief, but still unable to rest. The fate of Morgo, his most trusted advisor, was in the hands of Galena. He knew if anyone would be able to restore Morgo to good health, it was her, but even then, his chances weren't good. What was worse was Galena ordered them to leave her in peace while she worked on Morgo. She clearly needed complete concentration. She also assured them she would come to them when she was done. In Tark's mind, that meant he needed to stay close by.

He met with his remaining generals and found that many were hurt, but nothing major. Nina had a broken arm, Naradin a broken foot. Morak had suffered a painful burn on his arm from his own arrow. If Tark hadn't been so worried about Morgo, he would have laughed at his old friend. Yeia and Zaza both suffered deep cuts to the face and Weila was limping badly from a sprained ankle. Other than that, the remaining generals were fine. Tark sent them out to find out the overall condition of the elves and to report back with the information as well as news from the patrols set up around the camp.

Elenio was sitting on the ground beside the tent entrance, where he stationed himself shortly after exiting it. He sat crossed legged, his hands on his knees, eyes closed, and taking even deep breaths. Tark suspected this was an effort on his part to help Galena, but he was unsure exactly how it was helping. When he asked, Elenio continued what he was doing and ignored Tark completely.

Tark sat next to him, more to rest than to give him company. He was sure Elenio would continue to ignore him even if he did try to strike up a conversation.

"I brought you something to eat and drink," Taura said, bending down to hand him a tray laden with food and drink.

Tark smiled up at her, his eyes remaining closed. "How well you know me," he said wearily.

"More like how loud your stomach is," she said, sitting down next to him. "How is he?"

"Elenio or Morgo?" Tark asked his mouth full of cheese, fruit, and some type of bread.

Taura rolled her eyes at him.

"I don't know."

It had been several hours since he left the tent, a fact that had not escaped his notice. In the past when Galena healed them, mainly from injuries she caused during their trainings, it only took her a little bit of time. The fact she still had not emerged, did not bode well for Morgo.

"I don't know if she'll be able to bring him back," Tark said quietly, putting his tray on the ground, his hunger disappearing. "He was beyond repair if you ask me."

"I think the whole camp is waiting to hear. Everywhere you go you can hear muffled conversations discussing the outcome of Morgo, especially among the underground elves. Morgo was a very well-liked elf."

"You know he fancied Venia."

"Yes, and I think the feelings were returned judging by the progress she's made. What this will do to her, I am unsure, for she wasn't completely whole when we left." Taura began to draw circles in the dirt, she was struggling to keep her emotions in check for Tark's sake, but she didn't fool him. He reached over and took her hand in his own. In turn, she leaned toward him and he wrapped an arm around her, bringing her closer.

* * * *

"Elenio, I need to know what's going on," he said quietly.

For the first time in hours, Elenio opened his eyes and focused on Tark beside him. "I don't know. She has shielded me from her thoughts. I wouldn't be able to provide the peace she needs if I knew what she was doing or how Morgo was faring." Elenio looked around for the first time and noticing the tray of food on the ground helped himself to several items.

"You can't tell anything?" Tark asked, not believing him entirely.

"Hasn't Taura ever blocked you from some of her thoughts?" Elenio asked, before biting into a loaf of bread.

Tark had to think back and realized that there had been several occasions in which both Taura and he managed to block their thoughts from the other. It had always been when they had a surprise or were angry at each other. It was a simple matter of thinking of a structure encompassing their thoughts.

"Point taken," Tark said dully, looking at the quickly disappearing food on his tray before he realized he was starting to feel hungry again. "Hey, get your own food!" He pushed Elenio's hand away before he grabbed his third handful of food.

"I don't want to leave this area and I'm trying to help Galena out here. Why don't you go get some more and let me have this." Elenio, ignoring Tark's slapping hand, reached around and grabbed another piece of cheese.

Tark sighed and shook his head. He felt Taura's shoulders shake as she silently laughed at the two.

"I'll go get more food," she said, calming herself before she sat up.

"Thank you," Tark said wearily.

Elenio grabbed the tray from the ground and in record time, wolfed down the rest of the food. When he was finished, he lay it back on the ground and then resumed his meditation. Tark leaned back against the tent closing his own eyes, the events of the day finally catching up with him. The dark creatures had been so much more powerful this time around. It was all the elves could do to keep them at bay for as long as they had. Tark knew the intunerics fed Rau's power, but he wondered if it fed every dark creature's power and strength. It made sense that it would. He found himself vaguely wondering if there were any way Galena, with the Sword of Lumina, could destroy the evil stones. He would have to remember to ask her after she finished… He let his train of thoughts drop when the image of Morgo swam through his mind. Sadness filled him as he wondered if he would ever get the chance to talk to his inquisitive friend again.

"Tark." He heard a voice call him from somewhere above him.

Opening one eye, he squinted up, not that there was much light to keep out, and saw Nina standing above him along with Morak, Fala, Naradin, Hasa, and Zaza. He realized Nina was the one who spoke and broke his concentration.

"How are the elves?" he asked, groaning slightly as he got to his feet.

"Most escaped serious injury although the majority has some minor wound to claim. Between Galena and Nigora, we will need several days to recuperate from that last battle," Nina reported in her quiet voice.

"The enemy?" Tark asked, anxious to hear if Galena's fire barrier was holding them off, especially when her thoughts were elsewhere.

"The patrols reported a couple of earagos thought they could throw some of the other dark creatures over the ring, but when the fire rose up to meet the flying enemy, they discovered they were wrong. It looks as though they have retreated back to their camp," Morak reported, looking smug as he did so.

Well, that was one less thing to worry about.

"Have we heard anything on Morgo yet?" Fala asked quietly.

Tark just shook his head before looking down at the still, meditating form of Elenio. "She's blocked Elenio from her mind, although she seems to be using him for peace and calm," Tark said, still looking at Elenio and wishing he could see into his mind. Elenio grimaced at that moment, which caused Tark to crouch down beside him. "What happened?" he asked, panic in his voice.

Elenio's eyes shot open, wide and tear filled. He stood and looked at the entrance of the tent, to see Galena emerge. Her face was tear streaked and her eyes red rimmed. She looked dead on her feet and staggering, she walked over to Elenio before collapsing in his arms.

Tears, hot and angry, fell down Tark's cheeks as he remembered Morgo as he was. Wise and curious, always willing to listen to any crazy idea Tark proposed. He had fallen in love with the world above and was willing to go to any lengths to assure he would be able to remain in it. He had been the first elf Tark went to whenever there was an issue and he always had some sort of suggestion to help aid the situation. He'd guided them through the horrid underground world and joined the ranks of the elf army as soon as he was able. Morgo had been his calm when Tark missed his family the most and was so eager to learn any and everything in order to help them win the war. Could he really be gone?

Tark heard Nina sobbing softly and saw the tears in the other generals' eyes and streaming down their cheeks. He turned back to Galena who was being held up by Elenio. There were no more tears on her own face and she appeared to be holding on to consciousness. Her failing gaze traveled toward the entrance of the healing tent, causing Tark to look in the same direction. A hand was pulling back the flap and in a slightly broken motion, Morgo stepped out.

Elenio looked at Morgo, his mouth hanging open as was every other elf surrounding the tent. Morgo stood looking at them with a knowing grin on his face. He wasn't exactly the same as before. His grin was a little lopsided and his nose a little flatter. He definitely limped when he walked and his left side sloped a little. Nevertheless, it was definitely Morgo standing there, taking in all the dumbfounded expressions around him.

"Did we lose someone?" he asked, still grinning like a small child.

There was a collective gasp before everyone broke into wild cheers and laughter. Tark strode over to him and embraced the elf, whispering something in his ear.

Nina ran over to where Morgo stood, slamming into him when she threw her arms around his neck, causing him to wince slightly.

"Careful, I'm not sure if you know this, but I was just getting the grand tour of the Land of the Gods when I was called back."

The result was Nina broke into more sobs combined with laughter.

Elenio still couldn't take his eyes off him. He looked down at Galena and saw she had passed out. Which he expected with the amount of work she had done. It would have taken a whole fleet of elves to do what she did in several hours. He laid her gently by the tent where she wouldn't be trampled by celebrating elves. He had something he needed to say to Morgo and it couldn't wait another moment.

Walking over to Morgo, the other elves moved out of his way so his path was clear. Grasping Morgo's forearm with his own, he pulled Morgo to him and embraced him. He spoke quietly so Morgo was the only one who could hear what he said. "I owe you my life. If it hadn't been for you in that battle, I would have been the one visiting the gods and I'm not sure if I would have had enough strength to return. For that I owe you my undying gratitude." Elenio pulled back, put a hand on his friend's shoulder, and eyed him critically. "Whatever you need, I'll do my best to help out."

"I did what you would have done for me," Morgo replied, his expression changing from glee to a more serious expression. "It is you and Galena that I owe everything to. She told me before we exited what you were doing so she could concentrate better. Without you both, especially Galena, I would not be standing here. You owe me nothing."

Elenio embraced his friend once more, his relief so profound that it almost sent him flying. "It's good to have you back," he whispered.

"It's good to be back," Morgo said, the smile returning to his face.

"How do you feel?" Tark asked as Elenio took a step back and toward Galena. He bent over and scooped her up in his arms after assuring himself that she was only sleeping. He turned back to Morgo who was stretching his limbs in different directions to see if he had any limit to his movements.

"Stiff and some movements I have a feeling, will always be painful. My head hasn't stopped aching, but after Galena explained what she did, I'm not surprised. It is also painful to take a deep breath, but all together, not bad from the ordeal that I heard I suffered. I'll be curious to see if these new ailments stay with me permanently or if they disappear in time."

Tark burst into a raucous laughter before slapping Morgo on the shoulder, causing the poor elf to wince again. "Of course you're curious, it was one of the things I thought I would miss most about you," he said gaily.

Elenio excused himself then while the other elves made their way toward Morgo, anxious to tell him how happy they were to see him on his feet again. He needed to get Galena to bed where she would be able to recover from the tedious task she'd undertaken. After getting direction from an underground elf, he found the tent they constructed for him and Galena. Using her dangling legs, he moved the flap out of the way and entered. Inside looked exactly as it had at their last camp with a couple of chairs and a large hammock complete with blankets. Gingerly he laid her down and covered her up thankful Mira took her dreams from her. He hated to think of the nightmares that would await her if the goddess hadn't blessed her so.

Elenio pushed back her coppery hair and cupped her face gently, trying not to wake her. He felt the breath come and go through her slightly parted lips and sighed. He knew it was pointless to worry about her pushing herself too far as it never stopped her, but he did. This would be one of many times he would check on her often to make sure she was still breathing. Elenio pulled the blankets up and around her shoulders, tucking them in so that she would stay warm. Caressing her face once more, he pulled a chair over to the side of the hammock and sat down heavily on it.

What a day. What a year. To think it was almost a year ago when they had set out on this crazy quest. So much had happened, it felt as if normal was a lifetime ago. He watched her sleep peacefully, not wanting to leave her side until she regained consciousness. He thought of all they experienced on their journey; reliving the times he thought he lost her as well as the moments he had been most impressed and proud of her. Since leaving their village, Galena had become a whole other elf. She was always strong and beautiful, but now she was incredibly powerful and wise. She had learned more than any elf he ever knew in the shortest amount of time and had been through some impossible situations. She had grown into this incredible elf and through it all, she still loved him. He sighed thinking of their childhood and all the things they did together. Those were happy times and he found himself longing for them.

He awoke suddenly when he collided with the floor. He sat up gingerly, rubbing his head where he knocked it hard on the ground. He looked up to see if he disturbed Galena, but to his relief, saw she was still sleeping peacefully. She hadn't moved at all from the position in which he'd laid her. Getting up, he found himself startled again, jumping slightly when he noticed someone else sitting in the room with them. It was Morgo.

"How long have you been there?" Elenio asked quietly, taking a seat once more.

"For a little while. I didn't want to disturb either of you and it was nice to be able to sit back and enjoy the quiet for a time."

"Coming back to life not as peaceful as you expected it to be?" Elenio asked, grinning at his newly healed friend.

"No, it's not," Morgo said as he laughed quietly. "To tell the truth, I came here to escape from the others for a while. I do believe they feel I will disappear if they take their eyes off of me."

Elenio chuckled at his friend's attempt at humor. "What was it like?" Elenio whispered.

"What was what like?" Morgo said, looking intently at Elenio.

"The Land of the Gods."

Morgo continued to stare at Elenio for some minutes, his expression never giving away his thoughts. "Beautiful," was all he said.

Elenio nodded his head, understanding nothing more could be said about it. "Was it hard coming back?"

"I don't think I believed I really had a choice. I just knew it was the right thing to do," Morgo whispered. He shifted his intent stare to Galena's face and his expression softened.

"You know before we came out or I should say as Galena worked on me, she continually talked to me. Most of the time, she would describe what she was doing, I think to help her concentrate, but also for my benefit. She also told me about the cave."

Elenio snorted. "She hasn't even told me about all that happened in there."

"I don't think she thought I would remember anything she said. You know, I have searched for the kind of love the two of you have. Don't ever doubt her feelings for you. Remember this—she will risk her own life before she ever sees anything happen to you or any member of her family."

Elenio looked at Morgo who was continuing to watch Galena. He knew this about Galena, he had known ever since she left the cave and he had never questioned her love for him. "The feeling is mutual," Elenio said quietly.

"Mira took her dreams because of the images that haunted her from the cave. It was the only way to give her peace."

"She would wake up screaming every time and then refused to sleep. It got to the point where I thought I was going to have to knock her out for her to get any rest. With the Sword of Lumina at her side, I would have had to surprise her to do that though. It was hard for both of us the first couple of days. Then Mira came to her and she's been managing ever since."

Morgo just looked at Galena for a long while, his eyes never blinking. "Her talking of the cave and what horrors it held for her, confirmed my initial belief about the two of you. Like some commitment partners, one cannot live without the other. The two of you fit this description. You do realize where I'm going with this don't you?" Morgo said so quietly Elenio had to strain to hear him.

Guilt and shame welled up in Elenio and he couldn't meet Morgo's gaze. "I wasn't paying attention for some stupid reason. I let the death of one dark enemy go to my head and quit looking around or keeping my guard," Elenio muttered. He felt as though he needed to explain why he acted as he had.

"We would all miss you, but not even half as much as Galena would. You would destroy her and I'm sorry, but the fate of the elven nation rides on her shoulders. I'm not saying you did anything different than I would have, but please, be more careful with your own life." Morgo finished. He looked at Elenio solemnly, but Elenio could not meet his eyes.

"I'm sorry for what happened to you, for not doing what I have trained my whole life to do, for forgetting what's at stake. I won't make the same mistake again, of that I promise," Elenio said, attempting a grin as he did. "I can't promise I won't die and you can't hold it against me if I do, but I won't be so careless next time."

Morgo returned the smile. "If it makes you feel any better that great brute caught me by surprise too."

"Then why am I getting the third degree?" Elenio asked feeling slightly annoyed now.

"Because my death would not have left our sole means of survival shattered and completely useless."

It was in that moment, what Morgo was trying to explain, became crystal clear. After Galena, Elenio's life was the next most important life in the camp because of what it meant to her. He looked at Morgo and nodded his head, showing Morgo he understood now that guarding himself would save Galena in the long run.

"Now that this is behind us. Let me share an idea with you to see what your thoughts are on the matter. Tark brought up an interesting concept. Your dreams the night before, what did they consist of?"

Elenio was so startled at the shift in the conversation that he had to think for a moment before he could answer. He could remember they contained dark. In fact, he remembered being lost in the dark. He could hear elves screaming somewhere all around him and Galena moaning in pain, but he couldn't find them anywhere because of the extreme dark. He told Morgo all this, to which Morgo just nodded his head.

"Your dream is like most of the other elves I have talked to with the exception of who the loved ones were that were calling out to them. That changes from elf to elf. All of this confirms what I believe Tark has figured out. The intunerics have haunted us while empowering our enemy."

Elenio nodded his head in response to this. He heard Tark discussing that very idea with Taura while he had been meditating.

"Do you think it would be possible for Galena to destroy the stones then?"

"Yes, with the assistance of the sword, I do believe it's possible. My only concern is how many would she be able to destroy at one time. There are thousands of stones and it would take her entirely too long to reach out to everyone with her sword to prick it. My question to you is this, have you noticed her strength has multiplied since she became owner of the sword?"

Elenio nodded his head fervently at this. Not only was she always glowing from the power of the sword, but also she had become even faster and stronger since she first touched it. He saw she was able to accomplish bigger things now, like destroying a huge section of the enemy using several different magical methods, something she had not been entirely successful at before. Sure, she was able to use lightning, wind, and fire to do damage, but never all of them at once.

"That's what I thought too," Morgo said, noting the fever at which Elenio nodded his head. "I wonder if she were to use the same blinding light she used to chase Rau away from our first battle; if it would work with the stones too."

"I hadn't thought of that," Elenio said, scratching his chin while he contemplated the idea. "It could work."

"That's what I thought too. The best way to destroy the dark, even dark stones is with light," Morgo said, grinning at Elenio as he did.

"One way to find out," Elenio started.

"Yep, as soon as Galena wakes, we have her try it out."

Chapter Ten

Galena woke up feeling groggy and out of sorts. She blinked her eyes several times, trying to recall the events from the day before. Slowly, the memories started to return to her. She sat up quickly and almost sent herself flying to the ground yet again when she shifted her weight too quickly on the cursed hammock. If it hadn't been for Elenio catching her in mid swing, she would have embarrassed herself for sure. She looked up at him and smiled gratefully. He smirked at her, but it was the chuckling that caught her attention. She turned her head to find Morgo sitting in the chair opposite of Elenio. She studied him carefully. One side of his face seemed lower than the other and his grin was definitely a little lopsided. In fact, the entire left side of his body appeared to slope downward. Other than his looks, he appeared to be in good health.

"I see you're feeling better," she said sarcastically.

"Well, I definitely don't feel like I've been beaten within an inch of my life," he replied, his smile stretching across his face.

"What still bothers you?" Galena asked, feeling concerned now.

"Nothing to worry about now. We brought food," Morgo said indicating the large tray of food.

"Is that all for me?" Galena asked skeptically.

"Apparently, the elves who prepare the food remember you," Elenio said while trying unsuccessfully to keep from laughing.

Galena glared at him as he and Morgo burst into laughter. "I fixed you and I can break you," Galena threatened, but this only caused them to laugh even harder. Choosing to ignore them instead, she helped herself to several items on the tray and sat down on the ground versus giving them more reason to laugh by sitting down on the hammock.

Which, given her current record with hammocks, was very likely to happen. Her refusal to sit on it however, did not go unnoticed and it started both of them on a new wave of laughter. *Well, at least Morgo is alive and able to laugh*, Galena thought resolutely to herself. She continued to eat while waiting for the fits of laughter to subside and finally die away.

She took the time though to work on Morgo's face and left side while he was distracted. It gave her the perfect opportunity to fix his lopsided smile and straighten the bones and muscles sloping downward. She also noted there were several spots on his lungs that were not healed completely, which she assumed meant he had to have some discomfort when breathing. Although at the moment, no one would have noticed that. She searched his other organs with her mind; fixing all the minor details she had not been able to properly attend to when she had been repairing the majority of the more serious damage. Morgo turned to her when she finished healing some of the minor rips in the muscles around his biceps and took a deep breath. His eyes widened in surprise.

"How long have you been working on me?" he asked, surprise apparent in his voice.

"You were busy laughing and hadn't really answered my question when I asked earlier, so I took the opportunity to investigate my work from earlier. Why didn't you tell me you were having trouble breathing?" she asked accusingly.

Morgo's mouth hung wide open as he continued to stare at Galena in shock. Elenio just shook his head and grabbed a couple pieces of fruit off the tray. He was used to Galena taking mental notes of his physical condition.

"You didn't have to have your hands on me to know what was wrong?" Morgo asked, still looking stunned.

"No. You knew I could do that. That's how I was able to heal all the elves' ears," Galena said feeling a little annoyed with Morgo.

"No I didn't. My ears were healed by Nigora, I assumed that everyone else had seen her too or were suffering through," he said, still looking surprised.

"Oh, well, I discovered I didn't need my hands when I was helping Elenio after we started out on our own. All I really have to do is concentrate. Putting my hands on you just brings those ailments more into focus," Galena answered, shrugging. "Why?"

"I have never heard of a healer being able to do that before. They always have to use their hands to sense. How long have you been able to do that?"

"Shortly before I retrieved the sword. Afterwards, it became a great deal easier." She didn't understand what the big deal was, they already knew she could accomplish more things than any other elf had ever.

Morgo shook his head in amazement, before giving Elenio a knowing look.

Galena looked back and forth between the two, feeling like she'd missed something important. "Mind telling me what's going on?"

"It is just something that we were discussing while you were resting. I wonder if you would be willing to conduct another experiment for me."

"Some things just don't change, even with death experiences do they?" Galena asked shaking her head slightly at her friend's curiosity.

"Nope, not even then. Come with me." Morgo stood and waited for Elenio and Galena to follow him.

Galena stood and brushed her backside off and then her hands. "Lead the way."

Morgo stepped outside, and looked around, clearly not finding what he thought should have been there.

"Did you lose something or is this some nervous habit that I'm going to have to fix?" Galena asked, eyeing her friend curiously.

"Intunerics," he said simply. Even Elenio was looking for them now.

"I sent them crashing into the enemy army before coming back to help you," Galena responded, looking amused now.

"Well, that was a silly thing to do. You're making our enemy even stronger now." Morgo looked thoroughly put out by this revelation and crossed his arms angrily. "Bring at least one of them back until we see if our experiment will work," he demanded. Elenio too was crossing his arms expectantly.

Feeling completely at a loss now, Galena raised a hand and sensing the stones with the wind among the dark creatures; she caused the wind to strengthen and using it, reached down to pick up a particularly large stone. She heard loud shouts and bellows from the enemy as the rock flew past their heads and in some cases, into their heads and back to the elf army. She carried it over the fire where she stood, and placed the stone beside her, noting how she suddenly felt a great deal more depressed and tired.

"Why do you want this cursed stone back? They just make the elves sick and weaker. They fill our minds with dark thoughts, which, let's face it, we don't need any help in that area," Galena said, looking disgusted as she eyed the black stone beside her.

"We want you to try and destroy it," Morgo said calmly.

"Well, if that's all," Galena said sarcastically, rolling her eyes.

"Just listen," Elenio told her quietly.

"Elenio and I were discussing your power while you were sleeping and we both believe the Sword of Lumina has given you strength and power you did not have before. It has given you light in order to help you fight the dark," Morgo started, his eyes lighting up with subject. "I believe that you could destroy the stones much the same way that you were able to send Rau running."

"With the light?" Galena said feeling slightly confused.

"Yes. The stories say Rau was created from these very stones so it stands to reason, if you can hurt Rau with just a little exposure to your light, you should be able to destroy the intunerics with that same light. They do not possess the ability to flee from the burning brightness of its rays." Morgo's eyes were alive as he explained his theory to Galena and she smiled at him. She would have missed him sorely if he hadn't chosen to come back to them from the Land of the Gods.

"Makes sense," Galena said thoughtfully. "My only question is, don't you think the intunerics have more dark in them than Rau?"

Morgo looked thoughtfully at Galena for a few moments before answering. "No, because it took the breath of Haulua to make Rau what he is. I think they possess the same amount of darkness, Rau just has that little extra."

Elenio took Galena's hand and squeezed it gently.

"So you don't think by destroying it, we could be making more dark creatures?" Galena asked, still feeling uncomfortable with the idea of what they were doing.

"I don't know. That's why I only wanted to try it on one stone first. None of us know what will happen, but I still think it's worth attempting," Morgo said, scratching his chin thoughtfully.

"It won't hurt to give it a try. Then we can stand around and debate the outcomes," Elenio said quietly.

True, Galena thought. "Let me grab my sword. I seem to do better when I'm holding it."

Morgo's smile widened and Elenio held up a hand. "You stay put, I'll go grab it." He ran off in the direction of the tent, leaving Morgo with Galena.

"Do you really think this will work?"

"I don't see any reason why it wouldn't. As Elenio said, it can't hurt to try."

"What if it blows up and leaks dark magic all over the place?" Galena asked, eyeing the stone with suspicion.

Morgo thoughtfully stared at the intuneric while he contemplated this last statement. "All of these questions are interesting thoughts. We would be foolish not to expect something along those lines to happen."

"What do you think the worst possible scenario could be?"

"To have you destroyed."

"And you still think it's worth trying?" Galena asked skeptically.

"If you sense you're being overwhelmed, stop, or at least attempt to stop. If you would like, squeeze my hand and I will do whatever it takes to aid you. I'm not sure how, but I've been known to have a creative moment from time to time."

Galena was beginning to like the idea of this experiment less and less, but she knew eventually something would have to be done about the intunerics if they were to completely free themselves from Rau's reign. She took a deep breath and nodded. "Then you better get over here with me. Send me crashing to the ground or something if I squeeze your hand hard enough." She gave him a half smile before turning toward Elenio as he ran back to them, sword in hand. He handed her the sword, which she took gratefully. Galena felt the familiar energy of the sword wash over her and felt slightly comforted.

"Okay, let's get this over with," Galena said a little more nervously than she meant to. She grabbed Morgo's hand, to which Elenio raised an eyebrow. She shook her head quickly, relaying all that transpired in the short time he'd been gone with her thoughts.

Thinking of the same bright light she possessed when she was trying to get rid of Rau, she filled the entire camp with it. Many of the elves that had been walking around, stopped to shield their eyes, while many more poked their heads out of their tents, only to quickly retreat. Morgo and Elenio were both covering their own eyes, but surprisingly enough; the light didn't bother Galena. It hadn't in the valley either. She watched in fascination as the black intuneric slowly started to shake and then suddenly, as they had with the first earagos the sword pierced, cracks started to form within the rock.

Dark thoughts began to creep over Galena, making her cringe. *Why was she doing this? I could become so much more powerful if I used the stones for my own benefit. No, that kind of power only brought death,* Galena told herself sternly. Images of her loved ones dying replaced her thoughts of power and she dropped to her knees as they assaulted her mind.

The heart wrenching pain she felt within the cave gripped her and intensified to new levels. It crippled her. Tears poured down her face and she retched. She felt herself scream as the memories overwhelmed her. They were relentless, pounding her repeatedly until she couldn't remember who she was or what she was doing. She couldn't breathe. She didn't want to. She wanted to die. She eyed the sword in her hand and saw her way out. It would be easy. She could be with Elenio again. Gripping it more tightly in her free hand, she began to prepare herself for her final act when she felt an arm wrap around her waist. Alarmed, she looked down and saw Elenio's arm there. He was still shielding his eyes with one hand, but with his other, he held Galena securely.

He bent his head toward her ear, his mouth inches away. "Galena, I'm here. We're safe and together. It's the stones, you must destroy them," he whispered repeatedly.

Galena's thoughts returned to the present and a new wave of warmth spilled over her. She felt her determination and strength gain ground over the dark thoughts and she placed the newfound power in the blinding light, causing it to reach a brightness that made Galena squint her eyes. Within seconds, the stone shattered, sending chunks of rock everywhere, cutting her face and arms. Galena could see black wisps of smoke and something else drift up to the sky before disappearing altogether. Releasing the light, Galena looked around her and saw that the intuneric was gone. There was nothing left of it.

* * * *

As soon as the light faded, Galena released Morgo's hand and dropped to the ground on all fours. Tears flowed down her face in streams from the memories that consumed her for those few short moments. She took a cleansing breath and then turned toward Elenio, wrapping her arms around his neck and burying her face in his chest.

"I'm sorry," she cried.

"For what?" he whispered.

"For not being strong enough."

Elenio cupped Galena's face in both of his hands and turned her toward him so he could look her square in the eye. "You are never to apologize for that again. You are the strongest person I know. No one could do what you have done in just a few short months. Your biggest fear is not being able to protect us, which just shows me how selfless you are." He stroked the side of her face with his thumb, still looking her full in the eye.

"I couldn't have gotten through the cave without you and I couldn't have destroyed that stupid stone without you. How could I possibly be the strongest?" Galena sobbed.

"Because the strongest person is able to admit when they need help the most. Only the foolish tries to do everything on their own and they usually lose in the end. Never forget that." He pulled her to his chest once more as she fought to regain control again.

It had all seemed so real. If Elenio hadn't helped her through it, she was sure she would have given in to the thoughts the intuneric's dark magic seemed to plant within her mind. Even the sword's presence had not been able to ward off all the effects it had on her. It helped her, but Elenio's words gave her the strength she needed. She felt him gently stroking her long hair while he waited for her to calm.

"What if I can't defeat Rau?"

"If anybody can, it will be you. We knew, even with the sword, your chances would be slim, because he's still an incredible swordsman. However, at least he won't be able to use his shadows and dark against you. None of us knows the outcome of this, but we have to try. You said so yourself." Elenio said quietly.

"I know," Galena said, sighing heavily. "It was those stupid stones. It showed me the worst of everything and everything I saw in the cave. It even showed me what I have to gain by using the stones. It was horrible," Galena finished, shuddering as she did. No wonder the elves felt so gloomy around them. They were pure evil, solidified.

Galena finally turned to Morgo and his appearance shocked her. He too was on all fours and shaking badly. He reminded Galena painfully of what she felt like while she was in the cave.

"Morgo," Elenio called softly, noticing the elf for the first time as well. He let go of Galena and placing his hands on Morgo's shoulders, shook him slightly. "Morgo, are you hurt?"

Galena concentrated on him, but found nothing physically wrong other than his racing heart.

Morgo smiled weakly at Elenio, before sitting back on his heels. He placed his hands on his legs and fought to regulate his breathing. "I just need a moment. It appears that holding Galena's hand through the ordeal may not have been the best idea I've ever had." He closed his eyes, a tear trailing down his cheek as his breathing slowed.

"You saw what I saw, didn't you?" Galena said quietly.

Morgo just nodded his head, not saying anything more.

"I'm sorry." It was one thing to drag Elenio through her torments, but it felt completely wrong to have brought Morgo through the torture.

"Not your fault," he whispered back.

Galena crawled over to him and wrapped her arms around his shoulders.

"How you survived that cave is beyond me. No one else could have."

Galena squeezed him tighter, trying to hug the memories and pain away from him.

"You know what the worst part is?" he said, his voice barely audible. "I have never felt that passionate about anything in my entire life. That thought alone nearly caused me to take my own life. How can a person go through life without passion? If you hadn't regained some control, I would have ended it all."

Galena looked down and saw a knife at his knees. "Now, that would have been a shame seeing how I knocked myself out trying to bring you back," Galena said, smiling slightly as she pulled back to look at him.

"That's just it, I couldn't think past the pain. I didn't want to think past the pain. I only wanted it to stop. When you were finally able to destroy it, I realized I was holding my own knife at my throat."

Galena glanced at his throat and saw the beginnings of a slash. She quickly healed it. She had missed it before because she had been looking for something larger.

"And you thought you were weak." He laughed shakily.

Galena hugged him once more and then pulled back. "You came back from the Land of the Gods into a world turned upside down. Weak is definitely not a word I would use to describe you."

Elenio stood and helped Galena to her feet as Morgo closed his eyes once more. Taking another deep breath, which Galena was happy to see didn't seem to bother him as it probably had before.

"Well, one stone down, a whole land of them to go," Morgo said, smiling somewhat weakly.

"I'm not sure if I want to try that again," Galena said, wincing as more of the horrible memories that had been fading, popped into her head again.

"I wonder. I felt all of your emotions and saw everything that you saw. Did you see anything unfamiliar to you?" Morgo asked quietly.

"That depends on how often have you thought about using the intunerics to make yourself more powerful," Galena said quietly.

Elenio looked alarmed and turned quickly to see Morgo's reaction to this.

Smiling in an embarrassed sort of way, he answered, "Since arriving here, I have unfortunately thought of it often. When I woke up after you healed me, I noticed the thought perished so I assumed it had to do with my recent near death experience. Then Galena told us she removed the stones and I realized it was the stones placing those thoughts in my head. After this experience, I am left with no room for doubt on the devious nature of those stones."

"Since it was something I never even considered, I was able to easily dismiss the idea," Galena said, her eyes never leaving Morgo's.

"No, I don't imagine you would have had that thought. You have too much light in you for the darkness to corrupt you such a way."

Galena decided to rest and Morgo definitely needed to sleep after their ordeal. If she decided to destroy more stones, she would start on them only after she had gotten some sleep and food. She felt completely drained and didn't want to see anyone, but Elenio.

Walking hand in hand back to the tent, she opened the flap and stepped into the quiet dark of their accommodations. She took a deep breath, remembering Mira and what she did for her after her encounter with her nightmares. Elenio pulled her hand and spun her around so she was facing him. He wrapped his arms completely around her shoulders and kissed the top of her head. She buried her face in his chest and wrapped her arms around his waist, hugging him tightly to her.

"Once again, you were amazing," he said into her hair.

She gave a short bark of laughter that died out quickly. "That's not the word I had in mind for myself," Galena replied, burying her face further into his chest. "I'm tired of everything. I just want this whole thing behind me, but it seems no matter what I manage to do, more and harder tasks await." Galena felt a bone crushing weariness that hadn't been there before, seep into her very being. She hadn't realized how exhausted she was until she spoke the words aloud.

"I know." Elenio pulled her even tighter into his arms, making her feel warm and secure.

She just wanted to stay with him in here and not worry about the rest of the elven world for right now. She sighed heavily, content for the moment.

"What in the world was with all the light?" Tark demanded as he let the tent flap fall back into place.

So much for resting a moment. "Yes, I'm feeling much better, Tark. Thanks for your concern," Galena said sarcastically, pulling away from Elenio to sit down. She collapsed into the chair wearily, resting her hands on her legs as she regarded her angry looking brother.

"I assumed you were doing just fine when I was temporarily blinded by a light that could only come from you."

Elenio smiled and sat on the hammock facing Galena. He rolled his eyes dramatically so only Galena could see, but said nothing.

"We were conducting another experiment with Morgo. You know how he likes his experiments," Galena said, rubbing her eyes. They stung and itched from being so tired.

"What kind of experiment?"

"The kind where we use light to destroy dark intunerics."

"Did it work?" Tark asked anxiously. He stopped pacing and turned to look at Galena, surprise written all over his face now.

"Yes." Galena didn't feel like going into how the stones almost overwhelmed her mind with dark thoughts, and how close Morgo had come to being on the injured list again.

"I take it from the look on your face; it wasn't as easy as you thought it would be?" Tark asked, eyeing her critically.

"That's a minor understatement," Elenio said before Galena could even open her mouth.

Tark looked at him, nodding his head in understanding.

Galena leaned her head back on the chair and closed her eyes. She definitely wasn't looking forward to trying to destroy more stones any time soon.

"Hmm, that leaves me with a couple of choices. Nigora needs help with all of the injured elves, but less intunerics would leave us all in better condition." Tark started his pacing again, wondering aloud for Galena and Elenio's benefit.

"Let me help you out with that issue. It takes too much out of me emotionally to try to destroy any more dark stones right now. I'll put up a barrier of light around the camp and maybe that will help protect us from the intunerics until we're ready to battle again. Let's face it, everyone needs the rest," Galena said, still rubbing her tired, itchy eyes. "For now, I'll go help Nigora. We need to get as many elves ready as possible." Galena got slowly to her feet. What she wouldn't give for a little sleep herself right then.

Elenio watched her, eyebrows raised. She knew he was concerned for her and could tell how tired she was. She shook her head at him, preventing him from speaking his concerns aloud.

Mira's Last

"One thing first—a bit of good news actually," Tark said, placing a hand on her shoulder to keep her from leaving just then. "Nina just told me we have some visitors on the way. It seems more underground elves have decided to join us and they're bringing supplies."

Chapter Eleven

"How many?" Galena asked. She could feel a spark of hope in the pit of her stomach. Finally, something was going their way!

"Nina couldn't tell for sure, that's why I was headed here, before I was stopped due to a blinding light. Her best guess was at least fifty elves."

Galena looked at Elenio who was smiling broadly.

"Well, let's take a look shall we?" Galena retrieved a bowl from beside the chair where she had been sitting. She could make bowls from tree homes, but as she had discovered before, you couldn't make something if you didn't already have the necessary materials.

She filled the bowl with water and concentrated on the pale faces of the underground elves. It was difficult to do because she couldn't recall any of the facial features from any of them, as they had been so completely forgettable. Thinking more of the general appearance, she was able to bring up a group of elves walking quickly. She thought of herself flying back and instantly, the picture in the water started to change. The elves looked smaller and other features such as the landscape started to appear in the water. From what she could tell, the elves were moving at a very brisk pace. They appeared to be about a day's journey from where they were camped. Galena quickly counted the traveling elves twice, not quite believing her eyes. There were more than a hundred underground elves, all capable of doing magic, heading this way!

"Looks like Nina's count was a little low," Elenio said, still smiling broadly.

"Granted, none of them have been trained to fight, but they can help in so many other ways," Tark said, he too was smiling. "Did you notice all the sacks on their backs?"

Galena nodded her head, still studying the picture in the water.

"You know they can carry a ton of stuff in those sacks because of their ability to shrink it."

Again, Galena just nodded her head in response. "When was the last time that you checked with the patrol?" Galena asked.

"Just this morning, why?"

"Where is the enemy?" Galena saw understanding filling Tark's eyes and Elenio sat grimly back.

"They're starting to surround the majority of the camp from what the patrol can tell. It's somewhat hard to see past the fires. They only get glimpses here and there."

Galena emptied the bowl with a swipe of her hand. She placed the bowl back by her chair and strode out of the tent. *Time to check on the enemy*, she thought grimly.

Elenio and Tark followed her out and into the area surrounding their tents. Using the wind, Galena rose high into the air, high enough to see over the wall of flames that encircled the camp like a living barrier. She saw that the majority of Rau's forces were still within their camp, but several hundred had moved in around the firewall. They appeared to be testing the fire in different areas without much success. Some of the larger earagos were attempting to throw stones through the blaze. Galena thought of this when she first set up the flames and made sure to put up flickering wall of heat far enough from the camp that they would not be able to do any harm.

Seeing all that she needed to, Galena commanded the wind to place her gently on the ground. "They're circling the camp. There aren't very many all around us, the majority stayed in their own camp. But the underground elves are definitely going to need our help if they want to get in," Galena said more calmly than she felt.

Elenio crossed his arms and stared at the ground while Tark looked around him at the different elves gathered around them while Galena floated up in the air again.

"We need to put together a small group of elves to fend off the enemy while we get the underground elves to safety," Tark said thoughtfully.

"I can fly the group over and then when the underground elves come close enough, I can open up a section in the firewall and let them in."

"Can't you just fly them over when they get close enough?" Elenio asked.

"I've never tried to fly that many elves at once. I'm afraid something might go wrong or I might fly over some other unsavory creatures. I also have a feeling they may panic slightly when a wind they really have never felt a lot before coming aboveground, picks them up and tries to carry them away. I don't think I could keep them in the air if they fight it magically," Galena said, staring in the direction she knew the elves to be coming from.

"I think I need to talk to Morgo to see what his thoughts are on the matter," Tark said, scratching his jaw thoughtfully. "In the meantime, you might want to get over to Nigora and see if you can help out there for a little bit. Try not to exhaust yourself if you can help it. The way I see it, you're going to have to be a part of the small rescue team."

Galena nodded. She would have it no other way. Without another word, Tark headed off in the direction of Morgo's tent, leaving Galena, Elenio, and the large number of elves that had surrounded them, behind.

"Okay, see you later then," Elenio said under his breath.

Galena smiled before taking his hand and heading over to Nigora's. The elves parted to allow Elenio and Galena to pass. She could hear them whispering to each other as they, too, headed off in different directions.

"Have you noticed how none of the other elves really talk to me," Galena whispered to Elenio.

He nodded his head, continuing toward Nigora.

"Not even the elves from our own village."

"Have you made any effort to see any of them?" Elenio asked reasonably.

Galena smiled briefly at this. She hadn't. When she hadn't been in battle, she was solving some other magical problem or passed out cold from solving issue after issue.

"No, I guess I haven't really had the time," she said sighing heavily.

"I have and they're proud of you. A little surprised that Mira chose you perhaps, but proud."

"Have you seen Twoit since we left the last camp?" Galena said, so low Elenio needed to lean toward her to hear.

He shook his head sadly.

"I haven't either. She has never gone this long without turning up to at least get her head scratched or something. You don't think something happened to her do you? I mean, I haven't exactly been around to watch for her."

"She'll turn up, she always does," Elenio said quietly, giving her hand a reassuring squeeze.

Galena didn't feel reassured, but didn't know what else to do so she remained silent.

They arrived at Nigora's tent a few minutes later to find injured elves all over the place. They walked in and ran smack into Taura.

"Well, hello," she said pleasantly enough, although she looked worn out.

"What are you doing here?" Elenio asked, reaching a hand out and squeezing Taura's shoulder.

"Helping out where I can. Tark has been busy getting reports, talking with his ten most trusted elves, and in general, getting the elves ready for battle again," Taura said, looking around the tent despairingly.

"Where do you need me the most?" Galena asked, giving her sister-in-law a big hug.

"Where don't we need you would be a better question. The enemy really got the better of us this time. We almost lost a couple of elves, but Nigora managed to stabilize them until she had enough energy to work on them little by little." At this Taura gave a little smile, before continuing. "My job is to help keep everyone comfortable until Nigora can see them. However, the time between elves is getting longer and longer. The non-magical healers are doing all that they can, but it is very limited, as you well know."

"Well, let's get started."

Much later that evening, Galena finally had to call it quits. If she was going to be worth anything tomorrow, she needed a break. She sent

Taura back to her own tent once she found out the poor elf had been helping since late the day before. She also sent Nigora to bed for a long rest while Galena worked. All the other healer elves came in on different shifts and as Taura pointed out, were not much help without magic to aid them. Galena was exhausted. She'd seen at least a hundred different elves with every type of injury imaginable. Between healing and destroying stones, she had worn herself out.

Heading back to their tent, Elenio wrapped an arm around Galena's waist more to help her walk than anything. It had been an unbelievably long day and she needed all the help she could get.

"Why do you insist on wearing yourself out every time?" Elenio asked as he kissed her on the head.

"I don't know, but you would think that I would learn my lesson eventually." Galena tried to stifle a yawn.

"That will be the day," Elenio said, chuckling quietly. Taking his other arm, he knocked Galena's legs from under her, catching her in his embrace. He started walking with her safe in his clutches toward the tent. Galena thought of protesting, but a yawn nearly split her head in two. He hadn't gotten very far however, when Tark caught up to them, closely followed by Morgo.

"Is she okay?" Morgo asked, seeing Elenio carrying her.

"I'm fine. Elenio just thought I was too tired to walk." She leaned over and kissed Elenio on the cheek before he put her down. "So what's the verdict?"

"We have definitely decided against flying the underground elves into the camp without at least giving them the heads up. Morgo agrees with you on the fact that they would probably panic if a wind suddenly picked them up and sent them flying. But they're going to need help getting past all the dark creatures surrounding us."

"You must understand how extremely limited their knowledge is of this world and all the wonders it holds. Everything is relatively new to them and seeing that many dark creatures and then having wind pick them up, it might be too much for them to absorb at once," Morgo said, grimacing slightly as he recalled the world with which he was trying to escape.

"So how many of us are going over?" Galena asked, trying unsuccessfully to stifle another yawn.

"Well, you, me, my generals, and the some of their top elves," Tark said, as he ticked off all the elves that he named.

"And me," Elenio said quietly.

"That's fine," Tark said quickly. "The plan is for you to fly us over the fire wall so we don't leave the camp defenseless. We'll do our part to ward off the enemy while Morgo explains to the elves what will happen. We'll have you fly them over and maybe some of the elves can assist you in this area. Morgo was unsure if they would be able to manipulate the wind as they have no experience with it."

"Right, well then I need to get some sleep. When do you think they'll be here?"

"Sometime tomorrow morning, from what we can tell. Although, you would be able to help us out in that area..." Tark started.

"Then meet us in our tent first thing in the morning. She's done tonight," Elenio said, interrupting Galena before she could agree.

Tark eyed Galena, taking in her appearance properly for the first time since he had run into her. Galena knew she must look a sight. Not only was she extremely tired, she was also filthy. Other than the brief cleaning up she did after healing Morgo, she had not properly bathed at all in the last week. She felt tired and beyond dirty at this point. She knew she had to be covered in blood and gore from past battles and she could smell the sweat and dirt on herself.

"Very well," he agreed.

Galena nodded her head in thanks and allowing Elenio to wrap an arm around her waist once more, they headed toward their tent for the night. Before they entered however, Galena put up a brilliant, dome-shaped light. She smiled at the warm glow that it provided, feeling a great calm steal over her. *That should let everyone sleep in peace tonight,* she thought wearily.

* * * *

Tark was walking back to his tent when a warm glow surrounded him. He looked up at the sky and saw Galena must have put a dome in place just as she said she would. He smiled at it, feeling a weight lift

111

from his shoulders. All the dark thoughts of losing and what was to come, disappeared from his mind, replaced by Taura and Silva.

"I'll see you before the sun rises," he said to Morgo as he clapped his hand on the newly healed elf's shoulder.

Morgo nodded his head serenely, but continued to gaze at the dome overhead, the look of peace on his friend's face.

Apparently, the dome of light was having the same effect on everyone, Tark thought happily. He fairly ran to his tent, looking forward to seeing Taura as he hadn't seen her all day. Now that he thought about it, he hadn't really seen or talked to her since late the day before. With battles occurring frequently, Tark thought he had been acting very foolish indeed. He should have been spending as much time as possible with her, instead of wasting the time he may have left. She could have come with him to all the meetings and other tasks he had throughout the day. Just as long as they were together.

He could sense by her mood and knew she felt the same peace he did. Her thoughts that had been every bit as dark and twisted as his own, had smoothed out. Why they hadn't thought to use this dome before was beyond him. Tark knew this was exactly what all the elves needed if they were going to go against Rau's army and then on to Blackwell. Tark wondered vaguely if creating this constant light would further wear on Galena, but realized she kept the fire up without ceasing and it hadn't bothered her. Morgo had at one point told her the hardest part was setting up the protection, after that, the element was forced to stay in the same position until the one who commanded it, released it from the unnatural position.

Tark threw back the flap of his tent and walked inside. The pleasant light followed him in. Taura was asleep on the hammock, a hint of a smile on her lips. She looked too peaceful to wake. Tark sat down on the ground and simply watched her sleep. Her dreams dancing through his head. He saw his own image several times as well as Silva, Venia, Jamin, and several other of their new friends and family. His eyelids grew heavy while watching her. He stood up and stretched his stiff muscles. The exhaustion he had been running from the last couple of days finally caught up with him and he yawned, an act that made him even more tired. Carefully, so as not to tip both Taura and himself, he laid down on the hammock beside her. He pulled the blankets up and before even closing his eyes, fell asleep.

Tark awoke to someone shaking him gently. He opened his eyes, the light from the dome still glowing pleasantly within the confines of the tent. He blinked several times until the image of Galena came into clearer focus. She stood over him, a hand still on his shoulders, waiting to see if he was indeed awake.

"Time to get up. We need to check where the underground elves are," she whispered.

Tark slowly sat up, careful not to disturb Taura. Grabbing his sword and scabbard from beside the hammock where he laid it the night before, he followed Galena out of the tent and into the brilliant glow. His ten generals and their chosen elves along with Elenio and Galena stood waiting for him. The first thing he noticed were the smiles on all their faces.

"Did I miss something?" he asked, smiling himself.

"How do you feel?" Morgo asked, a broad grin on his own face.

Tark thought about it for a moment and realized he felt better than he had since arriving in this cursed land. His mind felt clear and incredibly well rested even though he knew he couldn't have slept more than a couple of hours. It had been such a sound, dreamless sleep it was all he needed.

"Exactly," Morgo said, taking in Tark's expression.

"Is this light wearing you down," he asked Galena.

"Not in the slightest. I can't believe I didn't think to use it sooner. When Elenio and I were traveling, we had to use this kind of protection to keep Rau away. I knew that the darkness couldn't penetrate the light."

"Well, you've had a lot on your mind too."

Galena's smiled widened in appreciation and she took Elenio's hand.

"Okay, so where are the underground elves?" Tark asked, getting back to business.

"They should be arriving within the hour," Elenio answered.

"Is everyone ready?" Tark asked eyeing everyone carefully as they nodded their heads enthusiastically. "Galena, do you think you'll be able to fly everyone over the fire wall?"

"Flying everyone over should be easy. It's going to be flying everyone including the underground elves back into camp that may be a bit challenging."

"You shouldn't have to fly all the underground elves," Morgo said thoughtfully.

"I thought you said they had no experience with wind?" Galena asked skeptically.

"That doesn't mean I can't show them quickly. I thought about it some last night, and I realized how foolish I had been in thinking that they would not be able to fly themselves to safety after they learn how."

"Do you really think they'll have enough magic?"

At this, Morgo almost looked insulted. "We have plenty of magic! You forget of all that we accomplished underground when we weren't worn out. You've just gotten used to seeing the underground elves here in camp. What you have forgotten is that there are roughly twenty underground elves using magic for close to five hundred other elves unable to do magic. We are in a constant state of being tired and as I'm sure you remember, makes it extremely difficult to accomplish a lot."

Tark watched as Galena turned several shades of red, before bowing her head in shame. "I'm sorry, I simply forgot. Would you like my assistance in instructing them in wind use?" she asked, humbleness in her every move.

"No, Nina and I should be able to manage. Your job is to keep the dark creatures away. Warfare is something the underground elves have had very little experience with. Generally only the guides for the tunnels learn how to protect themselves."

Galena nodded her head, but said no more.

Tark couldn't help it; he chuckled at Galena. She had gotten too big for her breeches and had been brought down a notch. "Let's grab some food and start heading toward the area where we will be flying over," Tark instructed. The elves as a whole made their way toward the food tent. Tark dropped back to talk with Galena while they walked though. "Will flying us break the light dome?"

"Light can be broken by anything solid. It just keeps the dark away," Galena said, looking at the ground as they walked.

"Still learning, huh?" Tark asked, referring to what happened with Morgo.

"No, just forgot. I won't make that mistake again. I guess I just got used to being relied on by everyone including the underground elves," she said calmly.

Tark chuckled again, and looking over Galena's bent head, saw that Elenio was smiling too. He had always liked him.

Tark sat down beside Galena while he finished the last of his sweet bread. She was already staring into a bowl of water with the image of the underground elves in it. They were moving at a fast pace and would soon be arriving at the point where they would need assistance. Galena set the bowl aside and looked around.

"It about that time?" Tark asked quietly.

She just nodded her head and got to her feet, adjusting her sword as she did.

"Are you nervous?"

"No, just ready to get started. I was never very good at waiting," she replied, smiling at him.

At this Tark laughed aloud and Elenio shook his head, laughing as well.

"No, you're not," Elenio said, still laughing at Galena as he pulled her into a hug.

Tark shook his head. Patient was never a word he would ever associate with his little sister.

"Alright, everyone spread out, but stay within this area. Line up several elves deep if you need to. It's about that time," Tark shouted out. He prepared himself by taking his blade out and twirling it around a couple of times. *Here goes nothing*, he thought.

Chapter Twelve

Galena felt the thrill of energy flow through her when she pulled the Sword of Lumina from its scabbard. It may not have looked like much, but Galena could feel the power in it and it never ceased to amaze her. She twirled the blade around a couple of times even as Tark and Elenio did on either side of her. She saw Morak and his group readying their bows and arrows and everyone else getting their own swords out. There was a nervous feeling in the air and Galena wiped her sweaty palms on her leggings.

The smiles faded from most of their faces as they all prepared for the battle that was coming. The biggest advantage they had was the element of surprise. Picking up her bowl she brought along just for this little outing, she focused on the image of the underground elves and found they had arrived within view of the enemy. She saw dark creatures of every kind heading toward them, evil grins on their faces. Looks of panic were on the underground elves' faces as they looked on in horror at the advancing enemy.

"Time to go," she shouted, throwing her bowl down as she did. Creating a great gale of wind that whipped around them, she brought the group high into the air. She felt the wind pick her up and send her flying high above the flames where she could clearly see the enemy picking up pace toward the underground elves. Looking from side to side, she saw she had been successful in bringing the other elves with her. She caused the wind to push them forward and over the blazing flames. The flames stayed where they were at Galena's command and let the elves pass harmlessly by. She brought them down on the other side and in the midst of the enemy who had not noticed them for their attention was still on the retreating underground elves. Galena picked up Morgo and Nina with the wind and sent them soaring over the heads of torlics, earagos, and many other creatures. She placed them gently within the midst of the underground elves. *That caught the dark creatures' attention,* Galena thought grimly as an earagos she had been running alongside turned and looked at her, shock written on his face.

"Hello," Galena said, smiling broadly at the shocked monster. She swung her blade up and around, burying it deep within the creature's calf. He roared in pain, stopping and turning to attack Galena. "Have I gotten your attention then?" She switched hands and twirled around. The earagos swung his giant club at her, missing her shoulder by just a hair. She twisted out of the way and around him, before the giant burst into light. "Forgot about that did you?" Galena said sarcastically.

She turned to see where Elenio and the others were and saw that they were doing very well holding their own. "See what a good night's sleep can do for elf morale," she said to no one in particular. She spun around, taking the head of a narook and cutting the arm of a passing torlic, both creatures erupting in light. She watched as Elenio flipped up and over a narook that was swinging his long fingers in Elenio's direction. Landing behind the creature, he stuck his sword into the narook's back. Using his foot, he kicked the lifeless body off before turning to see Galena. She smiled at him as he joined her in the fight. With backs turned to each other, they engaged several more creatures, Galena sending bolts of lightning in areas that were elf free as well.

She spun around swinging her blade at the advancing enemy and found her sword blocked by Morgo's own, "Oops," she said blushing slightly.

"They're ready," he said simply, before blocking the blade of a torlic that had joined in. The torlic however, made no further attempts at attacking, but fell over, an arrow sticking up from his back.

"Hmm, seems like I forgot to add fire power," Galena said, piercing the side of a dark creature that she had never seen before.

"That makes two of us," Morgo grunted while jabbing his own blade through the stomach of another torlic. "Keep the flames in check while I guide them over."

"Go," Galena shouted, eyeing two earagos who were stomping their way over to her. Elenio cut one in the foot, before spinning around and cutting deep into its leg. The giant roared, trying desperately to find the attacking elf.

"Down here, you great brute!" Elenio called savagely, before burying his sword deep within the back of his other thigh. The earagos swung his club around uselessly, always several seconds too late. Elenio spun around, jumped, and cut into the creature's hide with every move, finally forcing the creature to his knees.

Enthralled at the viciousness of Elenio's attack, she almost forgot to control the flame and at the last moment, remembered. Not a moment too soon from what she could see. The second earagos had also watched his own comrade fall to his knees before remembering that he was supposed to be attacking Galena, but just as he remembered, Galena pierced his leg with her blade. She could still see the surprised expression on his face after light replaced his form. She smirked, but her victory was short lived as two more dark creatures approached. Not wanting to waste time on them, she waved a hand causing them to burst into flame. They staggered around into other dark creatures, causing the fire to spread to whomever they touched.

Galena turned her head just as Elenio landed the killing blow to the earagos. He turned to look at her, a grim look on his face. She nodded her head at him, understanding his need for revenge. She turned to check on the progress of the underground elves and saw they all made it safely over the firewall and some of the dark creatures thought their chance had come and were trying to make it through the flames as well.

"Yeah, that's not going to happen," Galena said quietly to herself. Using the wind, she sent those creatures flying high in the air where bolts of lightning shot down destroying them.

Tark came up to her at that point, his own clothing covered with blood from the enemy and grinned at her. "You don't do anything half way, do you?"

"Now, what did father tell us about an injured creature?" Galena asked, blocking an oncoming blow from a torlic before sticking her sword into its gut. She turned to face Tark as the light bursting from one creature blinded the one Tark fought.

"An injured creature can still kill an elf," he grunted as he took the head off the blinded monster he was fighting.

Morgo came flying down between them, hacking away as he landed on Galena's right. Nina landed lightly on his other side. She too was cutting down a torlic as she landed.

"Have we had enough fun?" Morgo asked as he finished off a torlic.

Galena stopped, frozen in horror as she realized a problem with their initial plan; she had no way to distinguish between a friend and foe when flying them up and away.

"Umm, Morgo do you have any ideas on how I can distinguish who is an elf and who is a dark creature?" she asked, hacking down a narook while sending a torlic flying through the air.

"Yeah, look," Morgo responded as he swung around, blocking the blow aimed at his side.

"Brilliant, so how about when I'm trying to pick up everyone with the wind. I have no way of telling who is an elf and who is a dark creature. I can only sense a body and by the time I figured it out by using its size and shape that creature will have moved on." That their caught attention.

"Hmm, didn't think about that beforehand. I think it's time we brought our troops to you," Morgo said, looking around at all the fighting bodies.

Weila, Hasa, and another pair of elves were busily occupying an earagos some ways off and Morak could be seen fighting a narook with a sword, his bow strapped across his chest. Further off, Galena caught glimpses of other elves fighting against the tide of darkness that kept creeping in, but she was proud to see they weren't backing off.

"Start telling the elves to come to me. I'll grab them when I can."

Tark, Morgo, Nina, and Elenio nodded their head in unison. Tark and Elenio headed off in different directions, fighting their way toward their comrades. Morgo and Nina stayed behind and to Galena's amazement, began to fly elves one at a time to where they stood. Galena was impressed, but knew they would only be able to bring so many before collapsing. Reaching out as they struck a combined deathblow to the earagos, Galena scooped Weila, Hasa, and the other elves up with one swipe. She almost dropped them, when as one Weila and Hasa flipped so that their feet were pointing up and began to strike at the enemy from above. She had to give Tark credit for choosing them. Those two were ruthless when it came to fighting.

Galena brought the four over to where she stood and quickly explained what was going on while she concentrated on bringing another handful of elves over. Hasa and Weila wasted no time, but quickly got to work protecting Galena, Morgo, and Nina while they worked on bringing over more elves. Morgo flew Fala and two others over before collapsing to the ground. He was awake, but he was also useless now. Nina had also hit the ground, but she was out cold. Seeing the condition of them, Galena sent them flying over the wall of fire before continuing with the task at hand. Elenio and Tark had been successful at retrieving elves as well and were on their way back with several elves in tow. They were making a path of their own back to Galena.

"I can pick the rest up from the sky," Galena said to Erna who was blocking a blow from a torlic that was aimed at Galena.

He nodded his head wearily; sweat running down from his brow.

"Up we go." All the elves surrounding Galena and the ones that were making their way toward her, were swept up in the wind. She managed to pick up a couple of torlics as well, but with a wave of her hand sent them flying. *Wish I had had that idea a little while ago,* she thought dryly.

Apparently, Elenio had the same thought because he shouted "Umm, hello! You could have saved us a lot of trouble by doing that in the first place!"

"Yeah, I didn't see you offer any suggestions when I asked earlier," she called back.

To this, both Elenio and Tark rolled their eyes with exasperation. Galena sent them flying over the wall of fire while she brought more elves soaring into the sky. Anything evil and dark she sent flying in the opposite direction. Finally, after what seemed like an incredible amount of time to Galena, she could see no more elves. Sending a few lightning bolts in the thinning mass of darkness, she shot over the fire wall, landing a little harder than she intended on the elf side.

"Do we have everyone?" she asked as soon as Tark came into view.

"Yes."

"Good, because I don't think I could fly back over there if I wanted to." Galena sat down hard on the ground, her legs shaking badly and her arms hung limply at her side. "I need something to eat," she said wearily.

Instantly, one of the underground elves pulled out a small crumb of bread and grew it into a loaf, handing it to her when she finished.

"Thank you," Galena said, feeling somewhat taken aback.

"See and you doubted us," Morgo said. He was laying on the ground beside Galena, clearly exhausted from the amount of magic he'd used. Nina was on his other side starting to come to from her recent blackout.

"I already told you I was sorry about that. I had just gotten used to being depended on for what felt like everything," Galena said, biting off a hunk of bread.

Morgo just smiled and closed his eyes. "Yep, and I think I'll leave the flying elves to you for future reference."

"See what I mean, depended on for everything," Galena said grinning down at him.

Elenio came up to her about that time and handed her a flask of water, which she downed eagerly. "Well, we did it. We got all the underground elves in safely and they come with supplies. Remember those wonderful ires?" Elenio asked taking a bite out the apple he was carrying.

"Yep, they blow things up."

"They came loaded with them."

"Well, I say things just got a bit more interesting," Galena said.

* * * *

Galena devoured a couple loaves of bread before she finally felt better. She was still tired, but she had felt worse. Standing up, she thanked the underground elf once more when she realized that she vaguely remembered this elf. She tried to focus on him, but his face kept drifting in and out of her thoughts, reminding her of how she constantly felt the entire time she was underground. Shaking her head slightly to help her refocus, she looked intently at the elf who realized Galena was studying him.

"Are you surprised to see me?" the elf asked in the same dull monotone voice that was characteristic of all the underground elves.

"To be honest, I'm trying to remember if I've seen you before and I feel as if I have," Galena said struggling now to stay focused on the conversation.

"I am Lars, the head elder of Freeva," the elf said, smiling slightly at Galena.

"Umm, where was that again?"

"My village," Morgo answered, coming up behind Galena. He clasped Lars' arm with his forearm. "Welcome, my friend."

Galena stood back and stared with amazement at the difference between the two elves. She recalled a time when she had struggled to focus on Morgo, but now the complete opposite was true. Even with his slightly crooked nose now, Morgo was a good-looking elf. Everything about him had changed since arriving in the world above. Galena hoped the same would hold true for these new elves or she would really have a hard time getting to know them.

She left Morgo with his friend and went to find Elenio who'd wandered off in search of Tark. She wanted to go back to the tent and rest for a while, but didn't want to leave without letting someone know where she went. Who knew what they would do if they thought she'd gone missing?

She started heading toward the food tent, which was where the majority of the elves seemed to be heading, when she heard something strange. A high-pitched screeching or hissing. She couldn't tell which it sounded more like, only that it was making her ears ache terribly. She looked around and noticed several elves also seemed to have noticed the terrible noise as they were covering their ears in response. Galena looked around for whatever was making the sound, but saw nothing. She spotted Elenio coming toward her, his feelings of confusion racing through his and her mind.

Galena looked to the sky, but all that she saw there was the dome of light. She turned to look behind her, toward the wall of fire when the sound came again, this time louder and shriller.

Now Galena covered her ears as they throbbed painfully with the noise. Elenio was looking everywhere as well and many of the elves were crouching on the ground, alarm written on everyone's expression. Out of nowhere, a giant, winged creature came swooping down, snatching up an elf with one of its clawed feet. It went flying back up and through the light dome disappearing from sight. Another one shot down, snatching another elf from the ground before retreating to the sky. They moved with such incredible speed, that Galena was barely able to identify what they were.

"CRAGS!" she heard someone shout. She felt as if her stomach had been filled with ice as several more dropped to the ground with incredible speed, picking up more and more elves with every drop.

"I thought you said that nothing dark could go through the light dome?" Elenio shouted as they raced toward the nearest tent.

"And I thought I told you it would not keep anything solid out!" Galena shouted back, close on Elenio's heels.

"Galena! Take down the light dome, we need to see them coming," Tark shouted as he came into sight.

Instantly, the light was gone and what Galena saw almost caused her heart to stop. The sky was filled with the giant, winged creatures. Some of them now carried elves in their clutches, while others were eyeing the remaining camp with their giant black eyes. They reminded Galena horribly of a lizard that she would often find scaling the trees in her home village only a hundred times bigger and scarier. Rau used these creatures to deliver messages, but apparently, he had decided it was time they took a bigger role in the war.

Several more shot down toward the ground, snatching elves in their claws and retreating. Galena watched in horror as one of the crags grabbed Nina. It turned quickly before smashing into the ground before soaring back into the sky. Nina turned in its clasp and tossed something at it, within seconds it let go of Nina as it erupted into flames. She went careening toward the ground at incredible speed. Without thinking, Galena sent a gust of wind, grabbing her and bringing her safely to the land where she released the gale, placing Nina gently on the ground.

Galena raced out into the open, looking up at the sky to watch the Crags soaring high above, elves clutched in their grasp. Morgo joined her along with several of the underground elves.

"There is at least three or four dozen," Morgo said his face still turned to the sky.

"At least a dozen elves have been taken," Lars reported, a hint of emotion in his voice.

"We need to get them down before I can do anything to the crags. I'm afraid I might hurt the captured elves otherwise."

"Can you cause the wind to blow enough so they'll let go?" Morgo asked calmly.

"Worth a try."

Elenio came up beside Galena, sword ready. "You work on getting our elves back, I'll watch for any crags trying to sneak in," he said, watching the sky.

Galena glanced up, preparing the wind to whip around some crags, when more of the giant winged creatures dropped down, but instead of grabbing more elves, they deposited several dark creatures far from where the flames could reach them.

"Great," Galena heard Elenio say sarcastically. Tark had also arrived along with Taura, Fala, Morak, Zaza, and Yeia.

"Get those elves back and let us handle the monsters arriving," Tark said grimly.

Galena nodded her head. The sooner that she could get the elves back safely, the sooner she could make camp safe again. She turned her face toward the sky, focusing on whipping the crags around as she listened to the sounds of a battle breaking out around her. Just as Morgo predicted, several of the crags let go of their captives in order to right themselves. To Galena's surprise, another gust of wind picked up the now free falling elves and delivered them safely to the ground just as she had done with Nina. She looked around and saw several of the underground elves were guiding the wind with their hands. This act alone freed Galena up so she could focus more on releasing the elves and then destroying the emptied clawed creatures. Smiling, she turned her face to the heavens again, this time causing those creatures to burst into flames.

She grabbed her sword for extra strength as she attempted to shake more elves loose, but the crags seemed prepared for this. There were still a couple more elves being carried away by the crags toward Blackwell. She needed to act fast.

"Can you and the underground elves float the rest of the elves down if I get them free?"

"Yes," Morgo said.

Lars nodded his head in agreement and called for the remaining underground elves to join them in the clearing.

Satisfied, Galena took a deep breath and looked around for Elenio. She saw him battling a couple of torlics while Tark was dealing with a narook. She saw the few enemies that had been dropped off were quickly being dealt with. The crags were approaching with more dark creatures. Galena sent bolts of lightning after them, causing them to burst into thousands of pieces.

Galena sent herself soaring into the air at a speed she had only done once before when she had been joining the battle in the valley. She felt the wind whistle past her, it smelled of dark magic and death. Coming up to the first the crags, she cut the claw holding the elf off, allowing the elf to free fall before being caught up with a gust of wind. Galena raced past the crag, ignoring the final screech that it made as it burst into light. She caught up with two more, causing them both to burst into light with a swipe of her blade. The elves they carried found themselves swept back to the camp.

She looked down and saw she was flying over the enemy camp now and was heading directly toward Blackwell. The intunerics that were all around began to drain her. She felt her hope beginning to flee and dark thoughts taking over her mind. Weariness of a full day started to creep up on her. *Not yet,* she thought. She had to be quick with the remaining crags or they would soon be entering Rau's domain.

Sincerely hoping she wasn't about kill the remaining elves, she caused the remaining crags' heads to catch fire. This had the effect that shaking them with a second gust of wind had not had. Instantly, they dropped the elves, the fire that was consuming their bodies was also taking over their thoughts. The elves began to fall to the ground, and to Galena's horror, nothing picked them up. Apparently, they were too far away for the underground elves to help. Feeling incredibly tired, Galena created a funnel of wind, sucking up all the elves and some dark creatures into it. *They'll deal with them when they land,* Galena thought.

Her limbs were growing heavy and she fought to stay awake. She sent the funnel of wind to the elf camp, making sure to cause it to dissipate as it drew closer. Unfortunately, for those elves, Galena didn't have enough strength to make sure they had a soft landing, but were instead set down rather harshly. She couldn't help it though. Galena struggled to keep herself aloft and flying as she headed back to camp. The two acts combined seemed more than she could manage however.

She watched in a detached sort of way as the ground grew closer and noticed her flight had slowed down. The elf camp was still a couple hundred yards away. She could make it. The dark creature's faces started to come closer into view and still she was fifty feet away. *I have to make it,* she thought, her head rolling around as she fought to stay conscious. Twenty feet. The torlics began to jump up, trying to grab at her legs, which were just a little too high. She wasn't going to make it. She landed with a thud and took off running as fast as she could manage. The dark creatures were circling around her, menacing looks on their faces. Switching her sword to the other hand, she prepared herself to make a last stand. She saw the firewall just a few feet away; if she fought a couple, she could lower the firewall just enough for her to pass through. It was her only chance.

She turned and started to run again toward the firewall, cutting down the torlics that were determined to block her way. They burst into light, temporarily blinding some narooks beside them. Using this to her advantage, Galena ran past them, her legs beginning to feel like jelly and harder to control. Galena forced herself on. She heard another dark creature coming up behind her. Turning around, she quickly dispatched of it before resuming her race to the fire barrier. More and more creatures were coming. They all seemed to realize they had to beat her to the firewall.

A couple more steps. Galena started to fall, the ground racing toward her. She couldn't go any further. She was too tired. Blackness started to fill her vision when she felt it. Wind surrounding her, picking her up gently from the ground. She felt the sting of a blade cutting through the skin and muscles of her leg before the blackness consumed her.

Chapter Thirteen

Elenio examined the cut on his arm. It was a shallow one, but it still annoyed him. If he had been paying more attention, he would have never gotten it. The torlic simply snuck up behind him while he'd been watching the underground elves retrieve Galena. It wasn't a moment too soon, from what he could tell. She was already unconscious and bleeding badly from her left thigh. He'd just started toward her when he heard the torlic breathing behind him. He turned around, prepared to block him, but the torlic was already swinging. Elenio made to jump out of the way, but not quite soon enough. The torlic's sword ripped through the sleeve of his tunic, grazing his arm in the process. Elenio wasted very little time on the torlic after that.

He made sure there were no more enemies in the camp before he went to find Galena. The underground elves had taken her to their tent and made her comfortable. Elenio had also been pleased to see they had already healed her leg, which one of the underground elf healers indicated caused her to lose a great deal of blood in just a short amount of time. Morgo had been in the tent with her as well as Lars and Nina. Elenio nodded to each of them as a way of greeting before checking on Galena himself. He saw she was very pale, but otherwise fine.

"Would you like someone to take a look at that," Nina asked quietly.

"Take a look at what?" Elenio asked a little more harshly than he meant to. He was feeling rather annoyed at Galena once again. He figured he could feel that way now because she wasn't awake to scold him. *Might as well get it out of my system,* he thought sarcastically.

"The cut on your arm," she replied. She hadn't seemed to take offense to his shortness.

He looked down at the cut, but seeing that it wasn't particularly serious or painful, he shook his head. He would rather see the healers work on the elves with more serious injuries. Nina smiled at him and then beckoning toward Lars, the two of them headed out, leaving Elenio alone with Galena and Morgo.

"I should probably go and apologize to Nina," Elenio said, rubbing his eyes tiredly.

"There's no need, she understands," Morgo said calmly.

"Well, we did it."

"Yep, and not many underground elves passed out. Well, with the exception of Nina. I'd say we had a good day," Morgo said, smiling broadly.

"Want to go get some food? I'm starving. Plus, I want to talk to Tark and make sure no one was really hurt."

"I'm always game for food," Morgo said excitedly. "I've discovered it has a whole new taste to it in this world!"

Elenio shook his head at his friend. The small things seemed to amuse him the most. Morgo stood and following Elenio, and they headed toward the food tent. They passed a large pile of dark bodies, the only evidence of the crags that had dropped in the camp. Several of the underground elves were placing the glass balls filled with flammable chemicals called ires all around them and on them. Once they were satisfied all the dark monsters had at least one ires close to them, they set the pile ablaze with a white, hot fire.

"How many of those things did they bring?" Elenio asked as he watched the flames lick and dance all over the fallen creatures.

"Enough to get us to the end of this war come what may. We also have several elves who came just to produce more food, more healers, and a variety of other elves just willing to help however, they can. Tark is confident they won't be able to learn enough combat skills to be helpful during battle, but Lars and I are working on a way around that."

"I bet you have been," Elenio said, smiling and heading toward the food tent again. The smell of burning flesh filled his nostrils and made him gag. He was very quickly losing his appetite.

"Hmm, seems like we can send a breeze to clear away that smell," Morgo said thoughtfully. He gazed back at the blazing fire and seeing an underground elf watching the flames, he walked over to her. Elenio watched as they exchanged a couple of words before the female nodded her dark head quickly and with a wave of her hand sent a constant breeze over the fire, pushing the smell away from the camp. Elenio watched Morgo as he returned, lost in his own thoughts of Galena and what it would be like if he ever got to use magic. He wouldn't be nearly as helpless as he had been, that was for sure. Moreover, he wouldn't have to let Galena do it all, which was his biggest concern.

"What's troubling you, my friend?" Morgo asked, seeing the look on Elenio's face.

"Just wondering what it will be like when I can do magic for myself instead of complaining about everything," Elenio said, giving a half grin.

Morgo nodded his head, but said nothing.

"I'll be able to help Galena more. That way she won't have to risk her neck so much."

At this Morgo let out a bark of laughter. "I'd like to see you try and slow her down. She seems like she has always been a force of nature to reckon with!"

To this Elenio actually found himself laughing. "True story!"

"What's a true story?" Tark asked.

Elenio actually jumped at this. He hadn't realized Tark had come up on them.

"Your sister's whirlwind personality," Morgo said, calming down.

"Was anyone hurt?" Elenio asked, also settling down.

"Not seriously, and with all the new healers that have joined us, they've all been taken care of. With the exception of you I see."

Elenio shrugged this off and continued toward the food tent. The smell of sweet bread, juicy fruit, and something else delicious wafted toward him. He couldn't believe how hungry he was. Elenio smiled to himself thinking how hungry Galena would be when she woke up. He had better get his share now, because Galena was sure to eat hers and his when she finally roused.

"When you've grabbed some food, I want you to join me in my quarters."

Elenio and Morgo both nodded and grabbed some wooden trays.

A few minutes later, Elenio found himself sitting on the ground, food tray on his lap listening to the discussion going on. Tark brought all the generals, Lars, and a couple of the other underground elves. They discussed the ways the magical elves could help during battle. At this point, Morgo had plenty to say, Nina backing up everything said on the matter. Lars and the other two elves listened blankly to the conversation.

Elenio found himself tuning out the ongoing discussion and instead taking the time to study the new elves. There was Lars, another male elf called Wika and a female called Poro. All three had the drab, lank hair that was characteristic of an underground elf. Their pale skin seemed to glow in the dark confines of the tent and their dull dark eyes seemed huge in their thin faces. Looking at them reminded Elenio of how much the first group of underground elves that had joined Tark, changed since arriving in the world above. Galena pointed out, bringing out a jealous streak in Elenio, that Morgo turned out to be a rather dashing elf. Even Nina's once black looking hair had taken on a lighter brown look and was even beginning to curl. Her eyes remained dark, but they had a snap to them. As the weather grew warmer, Elenio noticed the once pale skin of the first group of underground elves was beginning to darken up so they no longer glowed in the sunlight.

"What do you think, Elenio?"

Elenio shook his head, trying to bring himself back to the discussion and failed miserably.

"I'm sorry. I quit listening right at the beginning. What are we talking about?"

He heard Fala and Erna chuckle somewhere behind him and he fought the urge to turn around and share their laughter. Tark rolled his eyes and Morgo grinned at Elenio.

"About heading out tomorrow at sunrise. We're just sitting ducks here. The longer we wait, the more chances we give Rau to strike out at us and weaken our already minimal defenses," Tark answered.

"So if you've made your minds up, why do you need to know what I think?" Elenio asked, feeling slightly annoyed. Why they invited him to this discussion was beyond him.

"Because I need to know what Galena would think on the matter and since she is currently indisposed at the time, we're asking you what you think on her behalf."

At this, Elenio raised an eyebrow at Tark.

Seeing Elenio's face, Morgo let loose a gale of laughter.

"Yeah, I guess that was a stupid question. I'm just trying to be official," Tark said, looking at the ground before bringing a hand up and through his hair. The rest of the group laughed then. It was almost as if a nervous tension was being released in that moment. Well, Elenio was glad he provided some humor to an otherwise extremely serious group.

"Now that the decision has been made, I think I'll head back to my tent and wait for the whirlwind to wake up. When she does, I'll let her know we leave tomorrow morning at sunrise." With that proclamation, the laughter died completely, replaced with a weighty silence. *So much for bringing comedic relief to the group,* Elenio thought grimly. He couldn't wait for this war to be over just so the fluctuation of emotions would end. One minute everyone was happy and gay, the next, reality set in, pushing happy thoughts out of the way.

He nodded his farewell to the group, grabbed his tray, and went to fetch more food for Galena. He expected her to sleep the rest of the day away and most of the night. He hoped it would be enough because tomorrow would bring the fate of the rest of their lives. One way or the other.

* * * *

Galena woke up to the thin light just before the rising of the sun. Her body felt stiff, and her leg was tender. Reaching her mind out, she found most of the cuts were healed, but there was still a great deal of bruising around where the torlic's sword cut her. She quickly healed the broken blood vessels there, easing the pain as she did. She sat up carefully, noticing Elenio still sleeping beside her. She looked around the tent, her heart aching slightly. It was in the mornings she missed Twoit the most. She could always count on the tiny creature's company first thing in the morning, but alas, the ferret remained missing. Galena sighed heavily and then spotted a tray laden with food on one of the chairs. Her stomach growled loudly, reminding her how long it had been since the last time she ate.

Galena got up as quickly as she dared and squatting down beside the food, she began to stuff in pieces of cheese, fruit, and vegetables as fast as she could. She filled her cheeks until they were bulging, chewed, swallowed, and did it all over again. Her hands were shaking from hunger and nothing tasted as good as that food. Taking a swig of water from a flask beside the tray, she picked up a loaf of bread when she heard a quiet cough from behind her. Turning, she found Elenio propped up on one elbow, a smile on his face as he watched her inhale an entire tray of food in just the few minutes she'd been awake.

"And then you wonder why everyone assumes you could put away half of the camp's food supply," he said with a mischievous smile on his face.

"Hey, remember what happened the last time you decided to pick on me for the amount of food I was eating?" Galena asked, while looking intently at her loaf of bread.

Elenio unconsciously rubbed his nose, the thought of bread flying up his nostril, front in his mind.

"Yeah, I thought you would," Galena said, smiling to herself.

Elenio stood up and walking over to Galena, took the loaf of bread from her hand, and returned it to the tray. He then turned to her and helping her to a standing position, kissed her lightly before holding her tightly in his arms.

Galena leaned her head on his chest, slightly confused at his actions. "What's going on?"

"Tark decided it's time to finish this. He figures the longer we stay here, the greater the chances are Rau will figure out a way in."

"He's right."

"I know he is, but you know what that means?"

"This is the last chance I may get to be held like this." Galena suddenly felt very sad and very scared. Everything seemed to be moving at the speed of light and suddenly she felt like she needed more time to prepare herself. Yes, the Sword of Lumina protected her from Rau's shadows and dark magic, but he was still an incredible swordsman. He defeated Lamiria with those same skills.

"You don't need any more time, you're already amazing," Elenio said, burying his face in her hair and kissing her head.

"What happens...?" Galena started.

"What happens will happen," Elenio said. Hooking a finger under her chin, he tilted her face toward him, his own eyes searching hers.

"I love you," Galena said. Three little words, but they told it all.

His own carefully constructed emotions broke for a moment, showing Galena the fear he felt before he regained control again. He kissed her, this time a little longer before breaking away. He held her away from him and just stared. Galena looked into his clear, blue eyes, studying them, memorizing them. The future was uncertain and she wasn't quite ready to face it.

"No matter what, we'll be together in the end," Elenio said, running a hand through her loose hair.

She nodded, knowing the meaning behind his words. They either both survived or they both would die, but they would not be apart.

"I need to get ready. Sounds like it's going to be a killer kind of day," Galena said smiling half-heartedly up at him.

He rolled his eyes and got to work on pulling his longer hair back. Galena focused on putting her long hair in a tight braid and polishing her blade with an old cloth. Her mind trailed back to happier times. Playing in the garden with her father and brothers; training with Elenio in the clearing by their village. Going to commitment ceremonies with her father and then with Elenio. Playing as a child with Elenio by the creek. She remembered all the things she loved and was fighting to maintain.

Elenio came up behind her and placed his hands on her shoulders. He bent down and kissed her head once more. Galena looked down at the Sword of Lumina and stared at the reflection in it. She saw her own coppery hair and her golden eyes staring back at her. She had changed since she left her village. Her face had gotten sharper, somehow fiercer looking. She saw a strong elf in that reflection, full of sadness as well as determination. What she saw in that reflection gave her the courage to stand up. She looked once more at Elenio, smiling briefly at him and then turned to head outside. The time had come to end this war.

Galena strode out of the tent and almost into Tark. He had been heading to her, to see if she was ready. He had the same expression as every other elf that was in the camp, determination mingled with the fear of the unknown.

"How are you feeling?"

"Like I'm about to throw up, so I'm good," Galena answered grimly.

To this Tark sighed, before pulling her into a hug.

"I think that's the general feeling that everyone else has."

"I'd say we're all set then. So what's the game plan, other than see an enemy and cut them down? Because although I'm sure that would work if we had less monsters to go against, but it lacks in the face of a storm."

Elenio shook his head slightly and ran a hand across his face in response to this.

"We're going to toss as many of the ires all around us and then between you and the underground elves, we should be able to give the dark creatures a proper hello," Morgo said, coming up beside Tark.

"Then you place a fire ring around the underground elves. They'll do what they can from within that ring, but at least they'll be protected. We can send any injured elves over to them for as long as we can, that way our forces will stay strong for at least a little while," Tark said looking around at the group of elves that were gathering. "Is there any way you can destroy the intunerics all at once?"

"Not without taking myself out," Galena said grimly.

To this Morgo looked down, red creeping up his neck. "They're made of pretty dark magic."

Tark nodded his head thoughtfully.

"I'll do what I can to move them as far away as possible though. That's got to help a little."

"Once we've made sure the underground elves are protected as well as we can, you lower the fire barrier and we attack."

"Does everyone else know what's going to happen?" Galena asked, eyeing the huge crowd that had gathered around them.

"Everyone was talked to yesterday while you were out," Tark said, also taking in all the elves around him.

Taura joined them, wrapping her arm around Tark's waist as they spoke. She looked up at Galena's brother, sadness written on her face.

Galena felt her own heart ache as she looked at her brother and sister-in-law. She looked around the camp, seeing for perhaps the first time, several elves from her own village. Faces of those she'd known growing up. There were faces all-around of the ones she loved and respected. There were faces there she'd never even made an effort to get to know, to even learn their name, but yet, here they were, prepared to make the ultimate sacrifice. Every one of them looked resolute and scared, preparing in their various ways to defend Tomiro from the creature who ruled them for so long. She saw swords drawn and bows readying. In everyone's hands, she saw at least one of the ires and some of them held more. Feeling moved at this final stand, Galena cleared her throat. Both Tark and Elenio nodded, realizing what she was about to do.

"Today is it. Whether good or bad, we put an end to this life, as we know it. We're all scared, but our determination is so much stronger. For lifetimes, we have been the slaves of that cruel monster. No more. We will show Rau what elves are made of! Today we will make Rau regret his very existence!" Galena used the wind to carry her words to all the elves. She watched, as they stood straighter, their faces looking fiercer. "Today, we take back Tomiro!"

To this, Galena met with a torrent of shouts from the elves around her. The sheer volume caused her to stagger, her ears ringing. Every weapon held high as the elves continued their battle cries. Galena turned to Tark and said just loud enough for him to hear, "Let's get this party rolling."

* * * *

The elves positioned themselves in various spots by the firewall. Underground elves were placed strategically between them, prepared to set the ires on fire when they encountered the dark creatures. Galena stood by Elenio, Tark, Morgo, and Taura. She held several of the ires in her hands. Her plan was to use wind to give them an extra boost before setting the small orbs ablaze. Looking to Tark, she waited for him to give the signal. He looked around the camp. All the tents had been removed and put away in the center of their area where the underground elves were to be stationed once the first part of their plan was put into action. Satisfied that everyone was where they were supposed to be, he looked at Galena and gave his head a short jerk down.

Galena returned the gesture and then sent a column of light into the air. On cue, every elf hurled their ires high into the air and over the fire barrier. Galena closed her eyes and listened for the resounding thuds as the glass orbs made contact with the different creatures surrounding them. Within seconds, she heard the sound she had been looking for. With a hand flung out, she caused the ires to erupt into flames even as she sent several more flying through the air. She set those ablaze too. The sound around the camp changed from a relative quiet to outbursts of pain as the dark creatures caught fire.

The underground elves were already racing back to the center of the camp, preparing themselves for the second part of their plan. Galena could see many more ires within their grasp and smiled. They would be throwing them out as the battle progressed into the swarm of black. That and they would be using the wind, as Morgo taught them, to fly injured elves to their side and to rid themselves of dark creatures from time to time. Morgo also suggested they use the wind to send heavier objects into the enemy, but Lars suggested this would probably not be a good idea, as it would wear them out much more quickly than they could afford. Galena agreed with him on this point.

Morak's archers took their positions toward the back of the lines and began to shoot arrows loaded with fire into the enemy army causing more shouts of confusion and pain to ring through the camp. They continued doing this while Galena set up a fire barrier around the underground elves. She knew it would be their best chance, but it still made her nervous to leave them that way. She would have to trust that their magical abilities would give them the upper edge.

Seeing they were all safely within the confines to the firewall, she looked around. There were still some elves lined up around the edges prepared to take on the creatures that surrounded the camp while the barrier was up. Morak's group sent several more arrows into this area and using bolts of lightning, Galena sent the rest of the creatures running back to the main group.

"Here we go," she yelled as loudly as she could. As quickly as the flames rose up, they went out, showing Galena and the elves the confusion their ires had spread. The enemy was running around in in complete disorder, some of them ablaze and colliding with others to spread the fire further. Not a single creature looked prepared for the elves to attack. As one, the elves surged toward the scrambling monsters. Galena grabbed the intunerics with a funnel of wind, sending the stones shooting out toward the dark creatures and far away from the camp. The stones caused further chaos among the dark army, which suited Galena just fine.

She met a narook head on as he scrambled to get his sword out. With one swing of her blade, she quickly dispatched of the creature. Elenio took on several more torlics and Tark joined him. Taura was busily defending herself against several other dark creatures Galena saw once before. Galena looked up and saw several crags flying high above and preparing to dive down on the elves. "Not this time," she muttered to herself. Sending another funnel of air up to them, she managed to suck up several of the creatures within the confines of the wind. Bolts of lightning pierced the funnel and when Galena released the wind, dead bodies fell to the ground landing on the enemy below and crushing them.

Galena looked around and saw they were pushing the enemy back. She felt a small twinge of hope blossom in her chest. Swinging her blade up and around, she cut deep into the torso of a torlic. She removed her blade and swung around again, flipping in the air to land in the middle of another group of dark creatures all in various stages of confusion. She dropped to the ground in a squat and spinning around, she cut off the legs of the creatures, causing them to crash to the ground before bursting into light.

Focusing again on the sky, she saw several more ires flying through the air and landing deeper within the dark swarming mass. Helping the underground elves out, she caused the ires to burst into flames when they landed. More confusion raced through the enemy lines and the elves took advantage of it. Like a giant wave, they crashed upon the monsters dispatching them quickly before pulling back only to crash down on them again.

Elenio came up beside Galena and together they fought on, closing the distance between the elf camp and Blackwell. Galena saw the dark castle growing bigger and bigger with every creature she killed. The smell of death and blood hung heavy in the air and the sound of screams and clanging swords filled her ears. She watched some elves soar through the sky and back to the camp, in various injured positions. The confusion that had consumed the enemy before was building as the elves continued their onslaught against them. Galena saw a couple more crags high in the air, circling around and looking for a good target. Galena quickly destroyed them by causing their heads to erupt into flames. Their bodies fell heavily to the earth almost crushing a group of elves engaged with an earagos.

"Ooops," Galena said quietly.

Elenio looked at her, shaking his head slightly and taking the arm off a nearby creature that reminded Galena of a torlic and narook combined. She shrugged her shoulder, watching several more ires fly through the air into a charging earagos before bursting into flames. She watched the giant creature stumble around blindly, crushing smaller monsters under his feet and causing many more to catch fire. An unfortunate torlic had gotten too close to one of its legs and was sent flying when the earagos staggered around and kicked it while he howled with pain. The smell of burning flesh filled Galena's nostrils and she suppressed the urge to gag. She felt hot and sweaty and still they fought on. They couldn't stop now, not while they had the enemy practically running toward Blackwell. *Time to move things along before we wear ourselves completely out.*

"Galena, pace yourself," Elenio shouted, reading her thoughts correctly.

She sighed before jumping up and flipping over the oncoming attacking creature. She plunged her sword into his back. Using her foot, she kicked the creature off, squinting her eyes as yet another creature became the victim of blinding light.

"I know, I know," she said feeling slightly exasperated. She caused a large funnel to form, much bigger than she had ever created and sent it roaring toward the enemy. She felt her hair whip around her, stinging her face and eyes with its lashes. Enemy and elf watched as the giant creation raced toward the monsters, sucking up everything in its way.

The elves gave a mighty cheer, yelling their approval from every direction. The enemy, on the other hand, ran screaming in the direction of Blackwell. The funnel rose higher into the air, growing thicker and thicker as the winds gained speed. The sound of its roaring drowned out everything else. Using her hands, she pushed the great roaring beast further into the enemy lines where nothing was safe. It left a clear path, showing the world exactly where it had been. Galena watched, her eyes alight with fury and power, the sword in her hand causing her to glow even more. Tark, Elenio, Morgo, and Taura stood next to her, watching the chaos unfold before them. Not a single dark creature was attacking, but instead was running in every direction, trying to avoid the ever-growing beast before them.

They crashed into the waves of the ocean separating the mainland of Tomiro from the domain of Blackwell and some raced across the bridge made of intunerics, trying desperately to escape. Bolts of lightning came racing to the ground to strike the fleeing creatures. Galena felt the ground tremble with the retreating monsters and the force of which her tunnel blew. She saw the wind column shoot creatures in every direction and causing others to collide with the ground below or into other fleeing creatures. It grabbed the dark stones that littered the ground and sent them flying as well, the results the same for everything that fell victim to this monster Galena unleashed. She began to feel the strain of trying to control such a large body of wind so she caused it to die instantly, dropping all the bodies within it to the ground with revolting thuds and cracks. She swayed precariously and Elenio caught her before she collapsed.

"What did I tell you?" he said angrily.

"I'm fine. I just need something to eat. I actually feel better now that I'm no longer trying to control that thing," she retorted.

"Fine or not, that was certainly something to see," Tark said, still looking at the place the funnel disappeared. There was not a creature within a stone's throw distance of them. They all fled to Blackwell where the remaining half of Rau's army awaited. Morgo handed Galena a loaf of bread and an apple, to which she nodded her head in thanks. She wasn't sure how he had gotten it there so quickly, but she found she didn't really care at that moment.

She stared across the ocean at the castle made from the dark intunerics. It loomed menacingly up to the sky ending in several jagged peaks. It reminded Galena of a set of sharp teeth pointing to the sky. The clouds above it were also dark and menacing, swirling around and around the top most peak. The water churned against it, continually slapping against the rocky base in an attempt to wash away this dark place. It hadn't escaped Galena's attention that this was the first time she had been to the ocean. The salty smell filled her senses with a clean refreshing feeling, only to be erased when she opened her eyes and saw the tarnish that it held.

The bridge that connected the mainland to Blackwell island was extraordinarily wide, roughly twenty elves could walk side by side across it and made entirely from the dark stone that was the predominate feature of this land. The bridge presented a couple of problems itself. The first issue that came to her mind was the fact that it was made from intunerics. Walking on those for even a short amount of time, could do a number on the elves and one Galena didn't feel they could handle just before battle. Sure, the elves were used to handling intunerics, especially when they started work in the mines, but being surrounded by this many was not a good thing.

The second issue Galena saw was even though the bridge was relatively wide; it still limited them like a funnel to the island. The enemy would wait at the other end and pick them off as they came across and tried to step on the island. Finishing her bread and starting on her apple, Galena brought up her issues with Tark and found he had been considering the very same things. He, like her, was unsure exactly what to do.

"Galena, why don't you cover the bridge in light?" Morgo asked, having listened intently to their concerns. Galena looked at Morgo, not really surprised, because he had so many good ideas.

"That could work," she replied slowly.

"It may not block all of the dark magic, but it will certainly ease it considerably."

"But there is still the problem of getting all the elves onto the island through a sort of filter," Tark said, looking back at the island again.

"That's a little tougher to negotiate," Morgo said thoughtfully.

"What if we do like we did when we first came out of camp?" Elenio asked.

"That would definitely get them to move back a bit," Morgo said scratching his head as he thought about it.

"Unless they're expecting it," Tark responded.

"That could very well be true, too," Morgo agreed, kicking a small pebble aside.

"Well, then we'll have to improvise," Galena said, throwing the apple core behind her. She heard a thump followed by an "ow." Guiltily, she turned around to see whom she had nailed and saw Morak walking toward them, rubbing his head in an annoyed fashion.

"Nice. Survive another battle, but get taken out by an apple core. Just how I wanted to end my fighting career."

Galena grinned sheepishly at him, feeling the heat rise up in her face.

"We lost a couple of elves and the ones that were injured are returning. The underground healers have done all they can today. In fact, most of them are out cold," Morak reported, still rubbing his head gingerly.

Galena looked down at the ground. This was the first time they had actually lost elves in battle. She looked ahead and knew there would be more before the day was out. She felt the weight of those lives heavy on her shoulder, but knew there was nothing she could do about it. They had all put their lives at stake, knowing the risks before they had taken them, but that didn't help her to feel any better at that moment.

Tark too was looking at the ground, sadness written all over his face. "Let's not waste those lives. Galena, are you ready?"

"Not in the slightest, but that hasn't stopped me yet." She would save as many elves as possible, but most importantly, she would show Rau what she was made of. Thinking of a bright light, she sent it sizzling down the bridge until the entire thing was covered in the same glow that protected their minds before. The bridge stood waiting for them, inviting them now to end the corruption at its other side. Tark raised a hand, gaining the attention from all the elves around him.

"To Blackwell. Let's finish this!" he shouted.

Chapter Fourteen

Galena stepped up to the very edge of the light covered bridge and took a deep breath. The first step onto the bridge very much felt like preparing oneself to jumping off the edge of a cliff. She casually tossed the ires a little way into the air before catching it in her hand once more. She looked to her left and saw Tark, Taura, Morgo, and nine of the fighting underground elves. To her right stood Elenio, Nina, and the remaining ten of the fighting underground elves. They had decided to join her at the front lines to help her with exploding the ires.

She looked at Tark once more to which he gave his head a brief jerk, indicating to lead on. Galena didn't respond, but started her journey across the bridge. Like Morgo predicted, the light didn't block all the dark magic, but it did help. Galena couldn't help feeling slightly more tired than she had been and depressing thoughts kept creeping up on her. Visions from Mira's cave kept floating around in her mind, but instead of making her want to turn back, they fed Galena's resolve, making her stand taller and feel more powerful. She would make sure her family and friends stayed safe.

The bridge seemed to go on forever and with every step, Galena's nerves felt as if they would burst from her skin. Looking sideways, she saw the same held true for all the elves. Elenio's thoughts and emotions were jumping all over the place to the point where Galena briefly considered blocking him. She was having enough trouble managing her own feelings at the moment. Tark's jaws were clenched tightly and Morgo looked more like he had when she had first met him.

Galena could see Rau's forces now. Just as they had predicted, they stood blocking the exit from the bridge. She could see hundreds of the bright, red torlics, the whip-like fingers of the narooks snapping this way and that. earagos stood menacingly above the rest of them, cruel smiles on their faces. She saw hundreds more creatures that never saw the light of day until Rau called them to war. Some had sharp spikes all over their bodies. Some were covered in an ooze. There were creatures with hundreds of eyes, and some with excessive amounts of limbs. Some looked similar to the torlics, but much more menacing because they were unfamiliar to her. All of these creatures together brought goose bumps to Galena's skin. These were the creatures created by the same dark magic nightmares came from, and all were various stages of horrible.

As the elves continued the passage across the bridge, several new creatures pushed their way through the mass of dark bodies to the front lines. It was the dreaded tookoos. These creatures Rau designed himself. They were the guards of Blackwell for a good reason. They were fashioned after Rau with the exception of being able to manipulate shadows. They stood as tall as the torlics. Their black bodies, blended in with the surrounding environment, making them difficult to see if you tried to focus on more than their outlines. They were incredibly powerful and very able swordsman, much more so than any of the other creatures the elves had fought against so far.

"How many of the tookoos do you bet I can take out?" Elenio asked Tark.

"Five fewer than me," Tark called back.

"Oh yeah, well I have six ires in my hand, so I think I'll have more than anyone," Morgo joined in.

Galena rolled her eyes. Leave it to her family to start making bets on how many they can take out before a big battle. "I think you all need your heads examined by a healer after this. You've clearly lost it," Galena muttered.

"I second that," Taura added.

Tark smiled crookedly.

Blackwell grew to huge proportions, blocking everything behind it from Galena's view. The land before it moved and shifted with anxious movements of all of Rau's army. It was an intimidating sight and Galena felt rather sorry it might be her last. *No, I mustn't think that way,* she scolded herself silently. The creatures at the end of the bridge were developing more features with every step they took until they were a mere twenty feet away. Stopping, Galena looked as menacingly as she could manage given her stressed out nerves. The monsters didn't look too intimidated. Galena wasn't sure how to feel about this, so she settled for just not throwing up.

"Ready?" she called. The battle cry of every elf in their army met her question. The shouts of all the elves caused Galena to shudder, pride swelling up in her. If she were one of the bad guys, she would feel a little nervous right about then. This however, didn't seemed to hold true with Rau's army as she heard snorts and laughter.

"ON MY SIGNAL!" Galena heard the discreet sound of hundreds of ires getting ready to be thrown. She knew for the elves toward the back to be able to reach the enemy with their ires, she would have to help them out with wind. She prepared herself to bring a gale up to accomplish that task among all the other things she felt she would have to do.

Instead of sending up a column of light like the ones she had in the past, she decided to get started with the enemy confusion and shot bolts of lightning from the sky into the biggest group of tookoos. She watched with great satisfaction as the giant beasts were blasted off the cursed rocks that they soaked so much dark energy from. The remaining tookoos looked a bit more alarmed and a great deal less confident than when the elves had first started their march across the bridge, much to Galena's amusement. *See, we are something to take seriously,* she thought smugly to herself. She looked sideways at Elenio and Tark and saw they'd noticed the tookoos reaction too, judging by the huge grins on their faces. Galena smiled as well. With the fleeing of the tookoos' confidence, hers grew.

"That was fun to watch," she heard Morgo call out from somewhere beside her.

We really do have issues, Galena thought.

She saw Elenio's grin broaden when he registered her thoughts in his own mind. "No, I think we've just finally reached our breaking point," Elenio shouted, still grinning mischievously.

"Are you two going to stand there and debate our craziness all day or are we going to earn our freedom back?" Tark joined in, tossing his ires in his hand lightly before preparing to throw it at the enemy.

"Nope, I'm good. Let's go," Galena answered back, shooting several more bolts of lightning into the black mass. With the last bolts of energy rushing to the creatures, the elves as one threw the ires at the shifting mass of dark creatures, helped along by a gale of wind. The glass orbs scattered throughout the enemy before bursting into liquid fire and spraying the monsters with flames so hot they were blue. Creatures collided with one another and ran screaming in pain only to meet other creatures howling with rage and agony. The chaos they were hoping to create filled the air as the dark creatures struggled to get back into their position with no success.

"ATTACK!" Galena screamed for all she was worth, feeling her throat strain with the effort. The elves ran at top speed meeting the chaos full on and finding no resistance. Elenio engaged a tookoo, staggering slightly from the strength of the creature's blows.

"By the way, I'm currently winning that previous bet," Galena shouted to him as she engaged several torlics and a dark creature with black skin and beetle like eyes that covered its entire head.

Using wind, she swept the torlics away and far into the ocean before engaging the dark creature that moved with incredible speed. Galena found its thousands of eyes allowed it to see in many different directions, giving it the chance to see things before they really got started. After attempting to cut into it several times with her sword, Galena turned as she set the thing ablaze.

"See that coming?" she muttered.

"I've got three down," Tark shouted somewhere behind Galena.

"I'm up to five," Elenio called back.

Galena just shook her head before using a blast of wind to remove several dark creatures from her path. She needed to get to Blackwell. She had an appointment to keep. Galena ran her blade across the backside of a charging earagos causing him to burst into light while she spun around, spraying liquid fire from her sword.

"That was new," Elenio said a little breathlessly as he came up next to her.

Galena looked at her sword appreciatively. She really needed more time to figure out what she was capable of with this weapon.

Tark and Taura came up beside her, engaging a group of narooks. One of the monsters managed to wrap its long fingers around Tark's neck, but his victory was short lived when Taura cut through his fingers. Galena came up beside them, destroying two more with a single swipe. Wiping the sweat from her brow, she looked around and saw the elves were pushing the enemy lines back.

The sounds of battle rang all around her. She heard grunts of elves as they swung their swords, attacking the enemy at every turn. She heard the whistling of arrows sailing overhead into the bodies of more dark creatures causing them to burst into flames. Galena fought on, growing more tired with every swing.

The castle grew larger with every fallen enemy until Galena could clearly see the main entrance. It looked like a large yawning maw in the middle of a monster's head. The thick wooden doorway was dark with age and corruption. It stood large and imposing, threatening Galena away with the dark secrets that it held within. It was through these doors that Galena watched with resignation as the one she dreaded the most stepped through and onto the landing. She stopped, staring at the creature that had ruled them for centuries. He was no taller than Fala, the tallest elf she ever saw. Muscles rippled through his shoulders, arms, and chest. His legs also showed signs of great strength. Shadows wrapped around him, swirling within his form. He was solid, but not, almost like his outer shell was made of glass showing everything inside. He seemed to move without really moving and the blade at his side was twice as long and wide as the Sword of Lumina, making it incredibly intimidating. His eyes searched the battlegrounds all around until they landed on Galena. It was time for her to make her last stand.

Chapter Fifteen

Galena stared at Rau. The coward was waiting for her to come to him. *Well, that's fine,* she thought grimly. Placing her sword in her scabbard so she could use her hands, she sent a fierce and strong wind straight to him, knocking down and blowing aside every creature that stood between them. The world seemed to stop all around her and all she could see and hear was him. Stepping into the path she cleared, she brought her hands up and over her head creating a ring of fire that sizzled all around her and Rau. Any dark creatures caught in the middle of the circle of fire, she sent flying with a swipe of her hand. The fire blazed all around, blocking out everything, but Rau. It wasn't as high as the one she used to circle the camp, but she knew it would do the job just as well.

"We finally meet," Rau said in his deep, guttural voice.

Galena cringed slightly at the sound of it, but refused to back down. "I believe we've met a couple of times before. Speaking of which, how's your face?" she said smirking slightly.

Rau's expression became distorted with anger.

Galena watched in fascination as he sent his shadows out toward her. She swiped her hand in front of her, sending out a bright light and causing Rau to hiss in pain. "Still haven't learned, have you? You can't touch me with your dark magic. You'll be forced to fight me."

"Shouldn't be much of a fight, you're just a silly, little female," he hissed menacingly.

"A silly little female you can't touch with your precious little shadows."

Rau sneered at Galena, switching his giant blade to his other hand as he descended the stairs that led to his doorway. Galena removed her sword from the scabbard. A calm stole over her as she held the Sword of Lumina in her hand. She swung it around and gripping it with both hands, prepared herself for Rau's attack. The swirling black mist making up his entirety was racing around within the confines of his body, showing the evidence of his anger. Galena found it hard to concentrate on him as a whole instead of the shadows within. Shaking her head slightly, she watched his slow progression toward her. She wasn't sure if it was the slow walk of confidence or the slow walk of fear, she was personally hoping it was the latter.

"You've caused me a great deal of trouble," he said, slowly circling around her, his blade pointing to the ground in his hand.

"Yeah, sorry about that. I was going more for the complete chaos type of attention. Apparently, I'm slacking." Galena followed his progress by shuffling her feet around; her own sword was still in both hands, ready and waiting. She realized she must look like a scared little elf, but she wasn't going to die trying to pretend she was feeling confident in her abilities.

Rau sneered at her once more, evidently he didn't like the way their conversation was going. Instead of saying anything else, he swung his arm up and arched it down toward Galena's head. She brought her sword up to meet his blade and was stunned at the strength of which he possessed. She slid her sword down the length of his before twisting away. She prepared herself again, secretly dreading his next blow. He didn't keep her waiting long, but came at her at a full run. Ducking down as he swung around, she felt the blade whizz past her head as she spun around, slicing his back. Shadows oozed out like blood from the shallow wound. Rau howled in anger, as he backtracked. Swinging around, he brought his blade up, cutting Galena's leg deeply. She screamed out, the cut feeling as if she had been burned with ice.

Not waiting for her to heal herself, Rau came at her again, which she managed to twist out of the way, flipping back so there was more distance between them. Using her hand, she sent out a blast of light toward him, which he managed to duck. He came running at her and spinning around at the last moment, struck her upper arm with a backward strike. Galena grabbed the wound, blood oozing past her fingers.

She turned so she was facing him once more, quickly healing some of the muscles there and in her legs as she watched him swing his sword in a circular motion before he came charging again. At the last moment, Galena jumped up and flipped over him, blasting him with bright light. Rau screamed out, blindly swinging his sword all around. Galena managed to skip out of the way, but just barely.

Her limbs were beginning to shake horribly, the pain in her arm and leg still burning fiercely. She focused on them once more, but had very little time. Rau had recovered. He turned to find Galena, his face more smoky looking than shadowy at this point.

"You know you'll never defeat me. Even King Lamiria couldn't," Rau said, his voice sending shudders through Galena.

"Yeah, I like to think I'm made of tougher stuff than him."

"I'll give you that." He closed the gap between them, striking down at her. Galena briefly blocked the blow, avoiding taking his full strength and dropping to a squat, spun around and kicked out her leg. She wasn't sure if you could knock down a shadow man, but it had always worked on Elenio. Her leg connected with his and she kicked them out from under him, causing him to land heavily on his back. She stood quickly, trying to take advantage of his awkward position, but he was too quick. He started to roll out of the way, but not before the Sword of Lumina could leave a cut in his side.

This time Galena followed, refusing to let him get to his feet without doing more damage to him. She brought her sword up, swinging it down to cut his back as he stood to his feet. She watched as her sword ran down the length of his back, leaving a gaping wound there. Shadows flowed freely from the cut, and she could tell it was starting to have the desired effect on him. Rau was growing weak and tired.

He turned around, switching his sword to his other hand, before coming at Galena full force. She blocked one blow and was sliding her sword down when he came back with blow after blow. It was all she could do to hold her own. She went to spin away, but he caught her other leg, cutting her calf almost in half. Galena was limping horribly, unable to stand on the injured leg. He came at her again, a ferocious look upon his face. Galena brought her sword up to block the blow, stopping it just inches from her face. She pushed up, causing Rau to temporarily lose his balance. She sent another blast of light his way, but he easily dodged this, running at her with full force. Galena barely got her sword up in time to block the blow. Using his sword, he managed to knock her blade away, leaving her exposed to his full onslaught.

"Mira help me," she quietly prayed. Instantly, a bright light filled the area within the fire ring. Galena felt her limbs grow stronger, the cuts healed, her energy restored. Using Rau's temporary distraction to her advantage, she flipped out of the way and picked up her sword all in one fluid motion. She turned to face Rau, who was wasting no time getting to her. She jumped up, and cut down with her sword, striking his shoulder, her blade biting deep into the tissue and muscles there. She landed behind Rau, facing him with her sword ready. His arm hung limply at his side, unable to grip his sword. He faced her then, taking his sword with his good hand. He was panting heavily and looked hesitant to attack again to which Galena smiled broadly.

She was preparing to charge again. Instead, was blasted to the ground with wind and light. Closing her eyes against the onslaught of light that could only come from a god, she waited until it faded, slowly getting to her feet in the process. Cautiously, she opened her eyes and seeing the brightness dimming, she looked behind Rau. Her stomach filled with ice as she beheld the god standing on the stairs directly behind him. Rau was doubled over, clearly feeling the toll of the wounds he suffered at the hand of Galena, not paying a bit of attention to the god behind him. This didn't bode well with her. She focused her attention on the god once more, noting the brilliant white toga and jet-black hair. He was impressive looking, if not handsome.

"To think, Mira chose to heal you versus keeping me in chains. I never said I had the smartest family," the god chuckled menacingly.

Unlike Mira's voice, Haulua's reminded Galena of everything she feared. She heard rockslides and roaring rivers bloated with the rain that fell all through the spring. She heard wild, angry dogs and the vicious voices of torlics. Her ears cringed with every word and she wanted desperately to clamp her hands over them, but thought that would portray fear. She stood straight and tall, eyeing the god with disgust.

"And to think she needed to keep you chained up at all," Galena said boldly.

To her surprise, the god laughed at this, but rather than sounding pleasant, it merely frightened Galena further. The god's laugh was full of cruelty and hatred. "What do you think you can do against me little one. I am a god, not to be trifled with."

She had to give him that one. Now that he was standing here, she wasn't quite sure what to do next. Nervously, she tossed her blade from hand to hand.

"So this is the famous blade that is supposed to be the downfall of my creation and me as well. Not much to look at is it?" he asked, eyeing the blade curiously.

"Yeah, neither is this place, but yet, it keeps attracting attention so something has got to be there."

"Fool," the god hissed, sending chills down Galena's spine.

She felt a great weight push on her from all sides until she felt crushed with the invisible force. She struggled to move, let alone being able to breathe, but her struggles were futile.

"Do you really think I need a weapon to destroy you? I can squeeze the life out of you without really trying."

It was in that moment, the voice of Mira echoed through her head. "The gods cannot directly take the life of a creature. It has be to done through others."

"No, you can't," Galena managed to gasp out, using the last of her air supply in the process.

"True, that I can't, but I can definitely injure you so one of my creations can finish the job for me."

The pressure intensified and Galena felt some of her ribs crack beneath it. Screaming in pain, the pressure released, allowing her to drop to the ground where she stayed clutching her sides.

"There you go, Rau. Do you think you can handle this pathetic creature now?" the god asked his creation sarcastically.

Rau grunted painfully, using his sword like a cane to stand straight. He looked wearily at Galena and seeing her crouched on the ground, sword lying beside her, and clutching her sides tightly, he grinned cruelly.

"Sure, now that I have been pulverized, you can take me on," Galena said just loud enough for him to hear. The act of breathing was painful enough, talking on top of that intensified the pain that much more.

Rau didn't respond to this, but took one slow menacing step toward her. Testing a theory, Galena reached out a hand and attempted to burn Rau with another ray of light, but just as she thought, Haulua blocked her attempt.

Yep, that's fair, she thought wryly. "Okay, I have one chance at this. It's time to show them what a silly female can do," she muttered under her breath.

Adjusting her feet so they were in a position where she could get up quickly, she briefly focused her attention on her ribs, healing them just enough so that she would be able to move without passing out from pain. She grabbed the hilt of her sword and felt a burst of energy she had not felt before. She looked down at the ground; still clutching her ribs with her other arm as if they still greatly bothered her. She listened for the sound of Rau's feet scraping over the dark intunerics that paved the ground. When he was just feet away, Galena said a quick prayer to the remaining gods and goddess. Quicker than she would have thought possible with broken ribs, she stood to her full height, shot out a hand and caused the face of Haulua to burst into flames. Knowing she had merely seconds before the god recovered from this minor inconvenience, she charged Rau.

The world slowed down, making every detail clear and distinct. She watched as Rau, using his remaining strength, brought his blade out and down at Galena. She could tell from the resigned look on his face that he fully expected her to block the blow. Galena, knowing she wouldn't have a chance at a fair fight, decided against doing exactly that, swung her sword down, readjusting her grip on the blade so she could bring it up and into the stomach of Rau with all the strength she possessed. She pushed the blade further into his body even when Rau's own sword cut deep into her side where it remained. The world righted itself as Galena stood, nose to nose with Rau, the tip of her blade visible just below the base of his neck and slightly above his shoulder blades.

"Not bad for just a silly female elf, huh," she spat, blood spraying his face as she spoke. Letting go of the hilt, Galena fell to her knees, her eyes never leaving Rau who stood above her, frozen and staring down at the sword. Galena felt his own blade still embedded in her side, but didn't have the strength to remove it. Hot, sticky blood flowed down her side, pooling around her in a dark crimson puddle. Her energy flowed out with it, and she didn't care anymore. She had done what she set out to do.

She saw Haulua vaguely in the distance. He had rid himself of the fire, but now stood frozen to the spot, dumbstruck. Galena would have laughed at the ridiculous expression on his face if she'd the energy, so she settled for staring at him with dying eyes. His own eyes remained focused solely on Rau.

Galena watched detachedly as shadows began to race away from Rau, as if they were finally free from their own enslavement. They seemed to drain away, leaving nothing but a black void in its place, much like an empty shell. All the features she feared and hated dissolved away as well. Tiny cracks, like a spider web, started at the point where the sword entered his belly, spreading rapidly through his body. They widened and grew, stretching out to the very tips of his fingers. Light began to peek out from those cracks, little bits at first, but then they began to shine out like beacons of hope. Rau seemed unable to move, to breathe. He stood, frozen like a statue, eyes glued to the sword that pierced him.

Haulua, who had not moved the during the entire process, reached up, grabbing fists full of hair, his eyes bulging in rage before screaming, "NNNNNNNNNOOOOOOOOOOOOOOO!"

Galena's eyes rolled back into her head, and her eardrums exploded with the cry of the god. She thought she was past the point of feeling pain, but clearly, this had not been the case. Blood came gushing out from both ears and down her neck onto her shoulders. She was too weak and tired to do anything about any of her injuries though. She found herself wondering how much longer she would be able to hang on.

Galena noticed the god's own body was covered in the same cracks as Rau, and light spilled from them too. The god took notice of these too and curses Galena had only ever heard from the angriest elves, flew from his mouth. She heard something about Mira and their mother, but decided what he had to say really wasn't worth listening to, so she tuned him out. An explosion of light and wind blasted everything on the island to the ground as both Haulua and Rau's bodies gave over to the unescapable light.

Her fire ring was reduced to ashes and the world around her lay motionless, as everyone was unconscious from the blast. Only Galena was left on her knees, her arms hanging uselessly beside her. She looked up to the sky, unable to control her head properly. Light came from every direction and nowhere at all. It blinded her, surrounded her, but still she could not shut her eyes. Tears streaming down her face, she watched as the dark intunerics all around her dissolved away into black smoke before dissipating into nothing. The very castle she found so imposing before shrank away, replaced by the blinding light.

Before her, stood three tall figures. In the center stood Mira, her fiery, red hair blowing around her as she stared lovingly down at Galena. On her right was a taller figure. He was incredibly handsome with bright, blue eyes and golden hair hanging around his shoulders. He had a sharp nose, but a gentle smile. On Mira's left was another figure every bit as tall as the blonde god. This one had dark, brown hair full of curls and falling just short of his shoulders. He wore a dark beard and had snapping brown eyes. He too smiled warmly down at Galena.

She tried to bow her head to them, but only succeeded in throwing herself face first onto the bare earth once covered by the hated, dark stones. She groaned painfully when she felt Rau's blade dissolve as well, leaving her wound gaping, and bleeding profusely.

"You have done well, my child," she heard the voice of Mira above her, but she couldn't look up, she didn't have the strength. She felt a warm heat spreading through her body and into her limbs, causing the pain of her injuries to fade completely. She took a deep breath, relieved that it no longer ached to do so. Using her hands, she lifted herself up until she stood in front of the gods.

"We thought our sister foolish to hide away a sword made of light. We didn't believe the elf race would ever return to their former state," the blonde god, who Galena assumed from the stories told was Luma.

"We are very glad to be proven wrong," the second god, Kya, said bowing his head to Galena.

"Peace, Galena. You have earned it," Mira said, her smile shining brighter than her brothers'. With that, they faded from view, the light fading with them, leaving Galena standing in the center of a beautiful island surrounded by light, all traces of Rau's dark domain gone.

Epilogue

In the instant Galena struck Rau with the final blow, every elf in Tomiro experienced a burning pain on the tops of their hands and the tops of their feet as the marks of Rau dissolved completely. Even the marks on the heads of every chief torlic dissolved, leaving the chieftain wondering why his race had decided to join ranks with the evil dictator. Dropping their blades, they returned to their homes where the now greatly reduced earagos, dwelled. The narooks, mauks, and tookoos also faded into nothing, having been fashioned by Rau with the help of the intunerics for sole purpose of controlling his slaves. The dark creatures that were never named had been created from the nightmares of elves and made real with the stones they harvested for Rau. Like every other creature born of the dark stones, they dissolved, following their creator into the empty void of no return.

In the following months and even years, Tomiro returned to its former splendor and glory. The elves began to use magic again, changing the world they once lived in to one worth living in.

Creatures that had long disappeared such as the favored pet ferrets, began to creep out of their hiding places and return to the elf villages. Twoit, Galena's beloved pet, was the first to make her grand appearance. She danced in delight the moment Galena crossed the unseen line of Blackwell's domain and the rest of Tomiro, much to Galena's joy and relief.

The remains of the elf army returned to their villages to reunite with their family and friends, spreading the tales of Galena and her triumph over the wicked god and his creation. The ones who perished at the hand of the dark creatures, were never seen again. Many believed the gods had taken these elves home with them, the ultimate reward for their sacrifice in the war against everything they stood against. Although their families mourned their deaths, they rejoiced in the fact they were so richly rewarded.

Tark and Taura returned to their village with their young daughter, Silva. It was there that Tark continued to train elves in the art of fighting. He never let the elves forget the terrible price of not being able to defend oneself against dark creatures. He believed it was his personal responsibility to make sure no elf was ever unprepared again, because peace would not last forever. He and Taura had many more children to add to their already precious family.

Morgo returned to find Venia. He was pleasantly surprised when she recognized him and even smiled. It was still many more months before Venia would completely rejoin the elf world, but when she did, she embraced Morgo and returned the love he gave to her. Her young son Jamin began to call out for Morgo as his dad, even before Venia came around. A year later, to Galena and Tark's utter joy, Morgo and Venia were united as commitment partners. They decided to settle down in Tomeka with Tark, Taura, Galena, and Elenio. Morgo helped Tark train armies, but spent most of his time working on the complete history of the reign of Rau so that future elves would never forget.

Many of the elves returned to their own villages to continue training their own family members with the exception of the underground elves. With the help of Nina and Lars, all but the oldest underground elves formed their own villages in the world above. Several of them traveled around Tomiro teaching elves from the different villages how to use magic more effectively as Morgo had with Galena.

Galena and Elenio finally went through the commitment ceremony with all their new friends and families present to witness the happy occasion. The celebration that followed lasted for several weeks, making it the longest celebration in the history of the elves. Together, Galena and Elenio created their tree home in the clearing where they used to train for hours at a time when they were younger. Galena remained powerful, with magical abilities that outstripped more than a hundred elves. Elenio, as he had threatened repeatedly, used his magical abilities to help Galena whenever the time arose, but also to get even with her for all the times she sent him flying through the air, into trees, and sending objects up his nose. For the first couple of months, elves refused to visit them in their home for fear of what would happen if they got in the way of Elenio and Galena's ongoing prank war.

Together, they had many children of their own. Their children also had magical abilities that equaled Galena's, much to Elenio's delight. He felt they were creating a new breed of elf that would be very hard to beat even without Tark's ongoing training. As to continuing with the sword, Galena decided she'd had enough fighting to last a lifetime.

Without the mines to wear away the life of the elves, their life spans continued to lengthen until they were practically immortal once more. The land of Tomiro prospered again, and was the jewel of the gods, by far their most beautiful possession. The greatest change evident by their enslavement was the elves' attitudes toward one another. In the days of Lamiria, grudges were common, and pride easily wounded, but after the triumphant return from lifetimes of enslavement, life took on a greater meaning. It was now nothing to take for granted, and forgiveness was a much more common concept. The elves never forgot what it was to wish for more time with loved ones, of a time when fear ruled and the desire to be with family was the strongest emotion possible. They no longer took their magic for granted, but cherished it as a skill to grow and something to always be thankful for.

As to the Sword of Lumina, it disappeared completely. Some said when Galena plunged it into the heart of evil; it dissolved into nothing, its job finally fulfilled. Others said Mira called it back, hiding it in the cave once more and making it available if the need should ever arise. Still others said that light can only be contained for a short time before it must go into the world to destroy the dark as only the light can do. Galena never knew what to think, but learned to accept it as a mystery just as everything was when dealing with the Sword of Lumina.

About the Author

I am a preschool teacher in a little town in Ohio. I have three wonderful children, Damon, Thomas, and Megan. I love watching football in the fall and swimming in the summer. Christmas is awesome and without a doubt, my favorite time of year.

Believe it or not, I did not like reading until about the fourth grade when I finally found a genre that really sparked my interest—fantasy. From there it became a passion of mine and often times the perfect way to escape the difficult times in everyday life. Mythical creatures are another love of mine so I combined my two loves and set forth to accomplish what I have always wanted to do: write books for everyone to love.

Facebook page: www.facebook.com/swordoflumina
Twitter page: @eelliottauthor
Blog Site: erinelliottwriter.wordpress.com

Also by Erin Elliott with Fire and Ice

Mira's View, The Sword of Lumina, Book 1
Mira's Hope, The Sword of Lumina, Book 2

www.ingramcontent.com/pod-product-compliance
Lightning Source LLC
Chambersburg PA
CBHW020645180626
46816CB00003B/1137